The Attack

Even the book morphs!
Flip the pages
and check it out!

Look for other **ANIMORPHS**® titles by K.A. Applegate:

The Hork-Bajir Chronicles

ANIMORPHS®

The Attack

K.A. Applegate

AN
APPLE
PAPERBACK

SCHOLASTIC INC.
New York Toronto London Auckland Sydney
Mexico City New Delhi Hong Kong

For Michael and Jake

ISBN 0-590-76259-1

Copyright © 1999 by Katherine Applegate. All rights reserved. Published by Scholastic Inc. SCHOLASTIC, APPLE PAPERBACKS, ANIMORPHS and associated logos are trademarks and/or registered trademarks of Scholastic Inc.

12 11 10 9 8 7 6 5 4 3   9/9 0 1 2 3 4/0

Printed in the U.S.A.   40

First Scholastic printing, February 1999

PROLOGUE

The dream came again. As real as it always was.

The Yeerk was in my head once more. He was starved of Kandrona rays, weakening, failing. I was watching him die.

The Yeerk cried in pain again and again. And the memory visions came floating up as clear as if they had all just happened.

They were visions of the Yeerk's life. And the lingering memories he had stolen from his hosts. One of those hosts had been my own brother, Tom.

I felt each of those minds in my own as the Yeerk gave up his life. I was the caretaker of those memories of despair.

At the end, the Yeerk was no longer in pain. He was beyond pain.

I opened my eyes and looked at Cassie. It happened so naturally. I opened my eyes by my own will for the first time since I'd been infested.

And then, for the first time in more than an hour, the Yeerk spoke. <So. You win . . . human.>

The Yeerk shuddered. I could feel it as a physical spasm. My vision changed. And I felt something impossible to describe. I felt as if I were seeing through things. *Into* things. Like I could see the front and back and top and bottom and inside of everything all at once.

It was as if I had slipped out of the normal world. Out of the real universe. I was in a different reality. I was peeking through a tear in a movie screen. On the surface, the three-dimensional movie — my world — played. Beyond it . . . something my mind could not comprehend.

In my dream, my dream of memory, I felt the terror grow. I knew what was coming next. I writhed in my sleep, twisting my sheets around me. *Wake up! Wake up!*

But I could not wake up. I never could, not till the dream was complete.

And so I saw it again.

A creature. Or a machine. Some combination of both. It had no arms. It sat still, as if it were bolted down, on a throne that was miles high. It could not move, and yet the power that flowed from it was like a hurricane of energy.

Its head was a single eye. The eye turned slowly . . . left . . . right . . .

I trembled. I prayed it would not look my way.

And then it saw me.

The eye, the bloodred eye, looked straight at me.

Through me.

It saw me.

It SAW me!

No! NO! I cried in silent terror. I tried to look away, but my eyelids were transparent, my head would not twist far enough to avoid its gaze.

It spoke the single word it spoke only in my dreams.

And now, at last, I could awaken, shaking in a sweat-soaked bed.

Why? Why would this dream not go away? I'd had other nightmares, other awful memories of fear and violence that needed to be exorcized in my dreams.

But they had each faded. While this dream came again and again.

I got up and staggered into the bathroom. I snapped on the glaring fluorescent light. Then I stepped to the sink and looked at my face, my head.

Yes, the Yeerk had died there, in that head, my head. It had been right then as the Yeerk disengaged and began to crawl out of me, right then as death closed its jaws around the Yeerk, that the eye had found me.

It had seen me.

And I had seen it. Then, and again in my nightmares. Again and again. And each time it spoke that single, voiceless word.

"Soon."

CHAPTER 1

My name is Jake.

Who am I? Sometimes I wonder.

I'm a kid, a middle-school kid, a kid with classes to attend and homework to do and friends to hang with and parents. I am just an average kid, at least on the surface. Normal. Boring, even.

I'm not especially good at school. I do okay. I'm no great athlete. I'm not some kind of genius. Just a kid. If you saw me at the mall you wouldn't think there was anything remarkable about me.

But there is.

Swimming around in my blood is the DNA of

1

dozens of animals. Birds, insects, mammals. The DNA floats there, encapsulated, waiting for my own mind to call it up.

And when I do — when I ask the DNA to go to work — it does, in the most amazing and impossible way. It transforms me. It changes me into the animal. Into the bird or insect.

I shrink or grow. I lose or gain strength. My limbs, my organs, my face, my eyes, all change. I become that creature.

My own mind continues to function. I am still me, but the animal mind is in there with me, too. And it functions, too.

So, anyway, about now you're thinking, *Oh, he's psychotic. He's delusional. He should be in a rubber room with an IV dripping tranquilizers.*

I'm not crazy. It's real. It happens. Not just to me, but to my friends: Marco, my main man; Rachel, my cousin, the war goddess; Cassie, the girl I care about more than I do myself; Tobias, the friend I couldn't save from his own bizarre fate; and Ax, an Andalite, an alien.

It's the Andalites who invented the morphing technology. Only they have it. Only they can take an otherwise normal creature and give him the power to become any creature.

Yeah, now I'm talking about aliens. Crazy and crazier, right?

But that part's true, too. Earth is being

invaded. Not openly, not with Dracon beams blazing and quantum explosives going off. That would be counterproductive. That's how humans might do it: fast and hard and obvious.

But the Yeerks aren't like us. They don't want our land or our resources. They don't want our pitiful, backward technology.

They want us. Us. Or at least our bodies.

They want our legs and hands. They want our ears and mouths. They want our eyes.

In their natural state, Yeerks are slugs who live in a liquid pool and absorb Kandrona rays for food. But evolution played an interesting trick with the Yeerks. Slowly, over the course of millennia, they grew to be a parasite species.

They found the Gedds, another species on the Yeerk home world. And over time they learned to penetrate into the very brain of the Gedds.

Gross? Weird? There's a species of wasp that lays its eggs in the living body of a caterpillar. When the wasps are born, they feed on the caterpillar. They eat the living caterpillar alive from the inside.

That's on good old Earth. So what's weird?

Anyway, the Yeerks expanded. From Gedds to Hork-Bajir to Taxxons to . . . us.

Now they are here. And now they are taking over human hosts, entering their brains, controlling them, rendering them utterly helpless.

3

I know. I was a Controller. I'd still be a Controller, except that my friends saved me and starved the Yeerk to death.

Not the first Yeerk death on my hands. Not the last.

We fight this war almost alone, me and my friends. We've learned of a race of androids called the Chee who help us from time to time. We've learned that not all Yeerks agree with the policy of expansion throughout the universe. And we know that off in space, outnumbered, outgunned, are the Andalites, fighting to push back the Yeerk tide.

But most days and nights, we are alone. Even with other people all around us, we are alone.

Assembly. Not a pep rally, not a drug lecture, not a ceremony honoring anyone. This was different, and actually, fairly cool.

The Lion King, the stage show, was in town. Some of the performers were there on the stage of our little auditorium to give a minishow.

A lot of kids had groaned when it was announced. You know: It was a lot of "be quiet, sit still" time. Not to mention the fact that it seemed a little "young" for us.

Me, I like quiet and still. Didn't used to. But now I guess any time I get to sit quietly, no running, no morphing, no terror, no screams, no horrible decisions and horrible aftermath . . . I can handle sitting still and listening to music and watching big giraffes gallop around onstage.

I was about fifteen rows back. Marco was in the row ahead of me to the left. I could see the side of his head, and he knew it, so he was amusing himself by twitching ears in time to the music.

I didn't want to smile, but it was just so idiotic it was funny. Marco, naturally, was hoping I'd snort or giggle so he could turn around and shush me, full of righteous indignation.

Cassie and Rachel were four rows behind me and to the right. I was pretty sure Cassie was asleep. Cassie lives an amazing life: school, the Wildlife Rehabilitation Clinic where she works helping injured animals, and of course, being one of us, which is a full-time job.

Rachel had a kind of dreamy look on her face. You'd have thought she was enjoying the show. Only I noticed the guy sitting next to her was trying to hold her hand. And that dreamy look was Rachel wondering which of the guy's fingers she should break.

I looked back at the show. It was a pretty good show. I heard a stifled yelp of pain coming from four rows back and to the right.

That familiar "Circle of Life" song started up and Disney animals were cavorting and singing and the music was swelling and Marco's ears were going nuts and a wounded male voice was saying, "Jeez, you almost broke my finger!" and then it all stopped.

All of it.

Every sound. Silence.

The music. Silence.

The actors in their incredible costumes. Frozen.

The auditorium full of kids. Dead still.

The only things moving were Marco's ears.

The only sound was Rachel saying, "Almost? Reach back over here again and I'll —"

Frozen. Still. Motionless. Everything and everyone.

Except the four of us.

CHAPTER 2

Slowly, cautiously, I stood up.

I looked at Rachel. "Wake Cassie up," I whispered.

Rachel stood up and shoved Cassie's shoulder.

"I'm awake, I'm awake," Cassie said, eyes snapping open. She yawned, then stopped in mid-yawn and forgot to close her mouth.

"Well, this is unusual," Marco said. "Did someone hit the 'pause' button?"

I was looking at the eerie spectacle of the stage players, frozen, some in mid-leap, just hanging in the air, when a blur of feathers simply appeared.

The red-tailed hawk flared its wings, yelled

7

<Aaah!>, banked hard right, saw me, saw all of us, and landed at the edge of the stage.

<Is he here yet?> Tobias demanded, wrapping talons around the lip of the stage.

I shook my head, confused. *Who? Was who here yet?*

One of the "animals" onstage moved. Only it was not a Disney animal. It had the body of a blue deer, the upper torso of a boy, a mouthless face topped by two extra eyes on moveable stalks, and a tail that could snap and leave you counting in base five.

Ax froze. Then he darted forward, moving away from the fake animals. Stalk eyes swiveling, tail arched, ready to strike.

"It's okay, Ax," I said. "I think."

<The Ellimist,> Tobias said.

Marco nodded. "I don't know anyone else who can just stop time whenever he wants. Unless it's that new math teacher."

"So where is he?" Rachel demanded.

"Wherever he wants to be," Marco muttered darkly.

We had encountered the creature — or creatures, who could tell? — called "the Ellimist" several times. He (she, it, they) was to humans and Andalites and Yeerks what humans were to ants.

I felt like an ant right about then. Small and powerless, with a couple hundred kids frozen around me. It was like they'd been videotape one minute, a still photograph the next. It felt wrong to look at them. Like I was some kind of peeping Tom.

I met Cassie's gaze. Her dark eyes were cautious, but not scared. The Ellimist had never hurt us. He'd helped us, always while pretending to do nothing. Or at least by living within his own incomprehensible set of rules.

One of the kids stood up. I jumped about two feet in the air.

It was this girl named Beth. No one else moved. Just Beth. She smiled at me, at us, and I knew right away.

"Yes, it is I," Beth said.

"The Ellimist?" Cassie asked.

Beth nodded.

"Where's the big voice and the quick-change bodies and all?" Rachel demanded.

"I have chosen this form for a reason," the Ellimist said in the girl's voice. "I come today on a humble mission. I wanted a humble form. One that would not evoke feelings of dread or awe or reverence from you."

He spread Beth's hands wide, palms up. He moved away, and I saw that the real Beth was still frozen in her seat. The Ellimist had not taken her body, just her image.

After all, he wasn't a Yeerk.

The Ellimist calmly walked through several rows of chairs and the bodies in them. Simply passed through them like they were air. He stood in the space between the front row and the stage. Down by Tobias. Ax came up behind him, moving with the unnatural, liquid grace Andalites have when they are preparing to fight.

Andalites don't like the Ellimist. He's a figure from the scary stories they tell around camp-fires — or wherever.

I gave Ax a little look, just a "take it easy" look. He relaxed about three hairs.

"Okay, so you're just a regular girl," Rachel said sarcastically. "No big show, aside from the fact that you froze time and all."

"This is as humble as I know how to be," the Ellimist said. "I come to —" he hesitated, "I come to tell you a story, and to see how you will choose to react."

"Oh, good, a story," Marco said. "Is it a musical, too? Will there be any *hakuna matata* involved?"

You have to understand: It's not that we weren't scared. We were scared. But we'd been scared by people who wanted to kill us. This was just "creeped out" scared. We ate "creeped out" for breakfast now.

Beth's face smiled. She had braces.

"I will tell you a story. You will tell me the ending."

CHAPTER 3

The Ellimist looked down at the girl's hands. "Once we had hands. Not much different from these." He smiled. "But that was a long time ago. Almost a billion of your years.

"We evolved as all living things do, some faster, some slower. We were among the first sentient species, but we evolved slowly. Still, given enough time, even slow change can become profound. Back when all Earth could boast were a few simple single-celled animals, we were beginning to watch the night sky and understand the movements of our own planet. We learned and we grew powerful. By the time worms first crawled in the mud of Earth, we were traveling in faster-than-light ships. And when the first dinosaurs walked we . . . we had become much as I am today."

"You'd become a girl with braces?" Marco said.

The Ellimist looked surprised. He showed the braces in a grin.

"The Andalites could do with some of the human sense of humor," the Ellimist said.

Ax scuffed a front hoof against the stage floor, a gesture of annoyance.

"And if the Yeerks had any sense of humor at all they wouldn't be the scourge they are," the Ellimist added.

Marco looked more abashed than proud. The smart remark had just popped out of him. I don't think he'd consciously planned to poke fun at a being who could not only annihilate Marco, but all memory of him, his family, and his ancestors, going back through a thousand generations.

The Ellimist continued. "We watched the rise of other species throughout the galaxy. Helped at times, when we could. We wanted companions. We wanted to learn. We imagined a galaxy filled with millions of sentient species, each with its own science and art, its own beauty.

"But it wasn't to be that simple. Approximately a hundred million Earth years ago, we became aware of a new force in the galaxy. Not a species, an individual. He was a fugitive from another galaxy, chased out of that galaxy by a power even greater than he. Greater than me."

"I thought you were all-powerful," Rachel said.

The Ellimist smiled. "No. I seem so only from your limited perspective."

I looked around the room. Time was stopped. Leaping dancers hung in midair. The dust particles in the air were standing still. A kid named Joey had been sneaking a Ho-Ho. Someone must have made him laugh because his mouth was open, smiling, and a piece of Ho-Ho was dangling off his lower lip. Dangling and never falling.

Powerful enough, I thought. I don't want to meet the guy who can kick the Ellimist's butt.

"This new force, this individual, began to make his presence known in our galaxy. And he had different ideas from ours. He sees a universe of conflict, pain, and terror. He craves fear. Not his own, of course, but the fear of others. He is a strange perfectionist, in a way."

The Ellimist had grown thoughtful. Perplexed, almost. Hard to picture when you were looking at Beth's bangs and the zit on her chin, but I knew who he was and what he was, and I guess I've had to get past judging anyone by looks. In a world where anyone could be a Controller, you begin to realize just how irrelevant looks are.

"He wants a galaxy cleansed of creation. His goal, I soon realized, is to destroy life. His method is to use one species against another, strong destroying weak, and then strong in turn being destroyed by the stronger still. He believes that there should be only one species. A single sentient race, which would be subjugated by him."

"What is this guy, a Nazi?" Cassie said.

Beth's curls shook as the Ellimist nodded. "In the moral sense, yes. But he has different visions of what constitutes total power. He wants to be able to control the strands of space-time itself. Not merely to see them and understand them, but to hold them in his fist and dictate the very laws of physics and nature, to recreate the galaxy in his own image, and someday to spread his power throughout all galaxies and destroy the one power greater than himself."

"Great," Marco said grimly. "Can we go back to *The Lion King* now?"

"He is called Crayak," the Ellimist said. And then he looked right at me, and I knew before he spoke the words. "You have seen him. And he has seen you."

The eye. The armless half-creature, half-machine.

One by one my friends looked at me, challenging, questioning, neutral, skeptical, compassionate.

"When the Yeerk died in your brain, you peered across the line between life and death; you broke the dimensional hold that blinds humans to things beyond themselves," the Ellimist said. "And in that moment, Crayak saw you. He saw that I had made myself known to you. That I had touched you. And he knew that you must, therefore, play some part in my plans."

Crayak. The nightmare presence had a name. Crayak. The bloodred eye that watched me in my dreams.

"Soon," it had said. "Soon."

I felt a chill crawl through my body. Fear. The Ellimist said Crayak enjoyed fear. Did he feel mine now?

"A hundred million years ago, we fought, Crayak and I," the Ellimist said.

And suddenly the auditorium was gone. We stood in black, empty space, and the Ellimist was no longer a little girl but a brilliant light.

CHAPTER 4

Stars, stars everywhere! Bright white points that burned with a steady light, and closer, so much closer, huge, sky-filling cauldrons of blazing hot gases.

His voice was in our heads now, reverberating through our bodies, huge and sad.

<I wanted to stop him, to stop his destruction. He wanted to eliminate me.>

As I stood on nothing, floating on nothing, stars began to dim and die. It was like watching a charcoal fire go from blaze to hot coals to crumbling, gray dust.

<The result was something neither of us could tolerate. The battle we fought destroyed a

17

tenth of the galaxy, millions of suns, millions of planets, a dozen sentient races.>

Before our eyes — or was it straight through our brains? — ran images, flashes of creatures in amazing shapes, in sizes and colors that made me want to laugh in sheer wonder. I saw monstrous mammals and tiny insects, species that lived in the sea and others that floated on air.

And one by one, they went as dark as their suns.

<A dozen sentient species, and more who would have achieved sentience, all destroyed, destroyed for nothing! But Crayak was damaged as well. The fabric of space-time, the software, as you humans would say, the software that runs the galaxy was damaged, twisted by the sudden explosion of our power.>

Once again I floated in that eerie n-dimensional space, the space beyond space where inside and outside were meaningless terms, where I saw the back as easily as the front, the heart of things as easily as the surface, the core of planets as easily as the crust.

I saw what seemed like threads, threads that could curl back inside themselves, disappear and reappear, twist and ravel and braid in insane complication.

<All Crayak's knowledge of space-time was now shattered. The few threads he had gathered

to him were yanked from his grasp. Millions of years of effort wasted. We fell back, back from our test of wills, our war.>

I was in normal space again. With guts and cores and threads all back where they should be, twisted up and hidden beneath the surface of things.

<We knew then, Crayak and I, that we could never make war again. Not open war, at least. The conflict would have to be carried on by different means. No longer a savage battle. Now it must be a chess game. There would be rules. Limits.>

Floating across our field of vision, like distorted TV pictures, were flickering images of our own interactions with the Ellimist. The times he had played a role, though never a controlling one. When he had shown us that we could escape Earth and live on a sort of game preserve for endangered humans. And when he had used Tobias to help some Hork-Bajir escape to found a free colony.

And when he had twisted time to return Elfangor from his happy life, hiding as a human, to a world of struggle, pain, and ultimately death as an Andalite warrior.

Elfangor, who was Tobias's true father, and the one who had given us our powers.

Each time, we saw the Ellimist limiting his involvement, refusing to do a billionth of what he could do.

<Earth is part of our game, Crayak's and mine. He would have the Yeerks absorb humans and later be absorbed by some still more vicious species. But Earth is not the reason I have come to you now.>

The show was over. We were back in the auditorium, not that we'd ever really left, I suppose. And the Ellimist was a girl with braces again.

"For millions of years we have played our game," the Ellimist said. "And we have lived within the rules, more or less. But now war threatens again. There is an impasse. A species I will not let Crayak take. A species he will not let me save. This species occupies a unique location in space-time. It is a turning point, and if Crayak can annihilate them, his power will grow, his goal become much closer, his forces become more deadly than ever."

"Including the Yeerks?" I asked.

"Yes, including the Yeerks, who will benefit from changes I cannot explain to humans — or even to mighty Andalites," he added with a gentle, steel smile for Ax.

<So what happens? Irresistible force and immovable object?> Tobias asked. <Who gives? You or him?>

The Ellimist said, "I will finish the story. And you will decide."

"Us?" Cassie blurted.

"Crayak and I have reached an agreement on a way to decide the issue. To decide the fate of the Iskoort race. If Crayak wins, they will be attacked, subjugated, and annihilated by another species."

<What species?> Ax asked.

"The Howlers," the Ellimist said. "You have heard of them before."

I nodded slowly. Yeah, we'd heard of the Howlers.

"Crayak and I have agreed to decide the issue by a contest of champions. His against mine. He has named the Howlers themselves, a group of seven. I am to pit my seven champions against his."

"What is this, a football game?" Cassie demanded.

"No, that would be eleven guys on the field, not seven," Marco said.

"Seven Howlers against my seven," the Ellimist said. "The winners — the survivors — will determine the outcome."

"And this has what to do with us?" Rachel asked belligerently.

"Oh, come on, Rachel," Marco said. "One . . ."

21

he pointed at me. "Two . . ." he pointed at Rachel. "Three, four, five, six," he pointed at Ax, Cassie, Tobias, and himself.

"That's six," Cassie said. "He needs seven. We're just six. That's not what he means. Is it?"

The Ellimist said nothing.

Cassie said a word I've never heard her use before. Then, "You want us, *us* to be your champions? To save these Iskrats?"

"Iskoort," the Ellimist corrected gently.

"I'm either honored or ticked off, I don't know which," Marco said hotly. Then, "Oh, wait, I do know which, and it's not 'honored.'"

"This must be your choice," the Ellimist said. "Yours alone."

He disappeared. Ax disappeared. Tobias disappeared. The four of us who remained were all back in our seats.

And time started up again, with dancers landing after the longest leaps of their careers.

CHAPTER 5

We sat through the rest of *The Lion King*. Seemed kind of dull after the special effects show the Ellimist had put on for us.

As soon as it was over, we were out the door. There was supposed to be a final partial period, but half the school was blowing that off, so we did, too.

We met at Cassie's barn, also known as the Wildlife Rehabilitation Clinic. It was a slow week at the clinic, I guess. Many cages were empty, which is rare. It made the place seem kind of forlorn.

Tobias was there waiting for us. So was Ax, in his weirdly attractive human morph. He

23

demorphed back to his own self. It didn't take any time at all for the conversation to start.

"This is nuts!" Marco said as soon as Tobias assured us that no one was lurking within earshot. "The most powerful creature in the galaxy, a guy who could make Earth disappear by just thinking about it, needs us to fight his battles for him?"

"Like we don't have enough to deal with?" Rachel agreed.

<The only possible reason for doing this is if it helps us in some way,> Ax said. <Enlightened self-interest.>

<I think we have that,> Tobias said. <The Ellimist has helped us before.>

Rachel shot him a dark, angry look. "He's tricked us before, too. Told us one thing and done another. We know nothing about him. We don't know if the Ellimist is one guy, or more than one. Half the time he says 'we,' then he says 'I.' So why is he *the* Ellimist? He jerks us around whenever it suits him, and he tells us squat."

I knew what she was talking about. Tobias had thought the Ellimist would return him to normal. Instead he merely gave Tobias back his morphing powers.

But that had not been a lie or a trick. Not really. He'd promised to give Tobias what he wanted. He had. It was Rachel who couldn't accept that Tobias had chosen, and still chose, to remain a hawk.

"Why does 'Howlers' sound so familiar?" Cassie wondered. "I know I've heard it before."

"It was the Howlers who destroyed the Pemalites, creators of the Chee," I said. "That's who we'd be going up against. Seven of them against seven of us."

"Seven? I count six," Marco pointed out.

"I think I know who our seventh would be," I said.

Marco rolled his eyes. "Erek?"

"Payback," I explained. "Who else would care as much about hurting the Howlers?"

Marco barked out a laugh. "He can't fight! He's an android programmed never to hurt anyone. He'd be dead weight. And why are we talking about this like it's time to choose up teams?"

<We hurt this Crayak, we hurt the Yeerks,> Tobias said. <The Ellimist loses, we lose.>

"Wait a minute, Tobias," Rachel said. "You know I don't run from a fight —"

"*To* a fight, maybe," Marco interjected.

"— but are we supposed to believe we're the Ellimist's only choice here? There's no one else in the entire galaxy who can go pound on these Howlers? Why us?"

25

<Yes,> Ax agreed. <Why us? Why not seven battle-trained Andalite warriors?>

This, of course, turned Marco around. "Excuse me? Like Andalites are badder than we are? What are we, wimps? Me in gorilla morph, you as you, let's go. We'll see who kicks whose butt."

"Yeah, that would be the sensible thing to do. You two fight," Cassie said dryly.

"Okay then," Marco said with a leer, "forget me and Ax. You and Rachel, both wearing bikinis."

Rachel calmly stuck out her arm and grabbed a handful of Marco's hair. "What was that you said? I must not have heard correctly."

"I refuse to answer on the grounds that you may tend to snatch me bald."

Rachel let him go.

<I'm starting to see Rachel's point,> Tobias said. <Why would the Ellimist ask for help from this clown college?>

"Could we win?" Cassie asked.

That stopped everyone.

She stepped into the center of the group. "Could we win? Could we save an entire sentient species? And maybe help ourselves, too? Maybe weaken the Yeerks in some way only the Ellimist understands? Seems to me that's the question. I mean, you know, I'm not Rachel. I hate fighting.

26

But the Ellimist put an entire race on the scale. An entire race. Maybe millions, maybe billions. And we're even asking ourselves if we should? How do you not at least try?"

"Iskoort?" Marco jeered. "Now it's our job to save Iskoort? What the . . . what is an Iskoort?" He looked at Ax, hands apart, questioning.

Ax shook his head. It's a habit he's picked up from us. Of course, he does it while holding his stalk eyes still, so it's a bit different.

<I have never heard of the Iskoort.>

Normally, on big issues like this I don't push my opinions out there. I'm supposedly the leader, but to me there are times when the best thing a leader can do is let others work things out for themselves. But I had to say something.

"I think . . . I think there may be something else going on here, with the Ellimist choosing us."

Everyone stared at me. Marco narrowed his eyes. "The Ellimist said something about you seeing this Crayak."

"I saw him. When the Yeerk died in my head, I saw him. And he saw me. And since then . . . since then I've had dreams."

Dead silence.

I wished I'd kept my mouth shut. "Look, I . . . you know, dreams are weird. Like who knows if they're ever real? But these feel real. And in the

27

dreams I see him. Crayak." I shook my head. "I know this sounds crazy."

"Uh, Jake?" Marco said. "We've been over the line into crazy since Elfangor said, 'Hey, kids, wanna turn into animals?'"

I smiled. That was not exactly what Elfangor had said. "I just feel like these dreams aren't totally just dreams. I see him. And he sees me. And he says the same thing each time."

"What?" Cassie put a soft hand on my arm. "What does he say?"

"'Soon.' He just says 'soon.'"

CHAPTER 6

"Ooookay," Marco said. "I felt *that* chill go up my spine."

"So what does all this tell us?" Rachel demanded. "This Crayak already doesn't like us, so we go and fight his handpicked team? Maybe win? Then he loves us? I don't think so."

<Side bets,> Tobias said.

I nodded. No one else got it.

<The Ellimist and Crayak have their main event: Do the Iskoort live or die? But maybe there's some action on the side. Us. Maybe that's why he chose us. Maybe there's another level.>

"What other level?" Rachel demanded, frustrated.

<I don't know,> Tobias admitted. <But here's the thing: It's down to Crayak versus Ellimist. Crayak already has it in for Jake, at the very least. Not to mention he backs the Yeerks. Not to mention we know the Howlers are just as bad. The Ellimist wouldn't pick us if he didn't think we had a chance.>

Cassie was nodding. She was for it. That made two.

I looked to Ax. He made the strange, mouthless Andalite smile. <If we can hurt the Yeerks . . .>

That made three. I looked at Rachel.

"Oh, come on, you have to ask? No Crayak space monster is gonna beat up on my cousin," she said, flashing her Cover Girl smile.

Down to Marco. He looked doubtful. I've learned to trust Marco's doubts.

"What is it?" I asked him.

"First of all, I'm in," Marco said. "But I just want to point out one thing: The Ellimist didn't force us, he asked us. Our choice. And maybe he's right that we can do this. But part of the reason we're saying yes is that this Crayak thing has been taking pokes at Jake. And Crayak plays the same long, patient games the Ellimist does."

"So what are you saying?" Cassie asked.

"I'm saying maybe Crayak wants us there.

Maybe he wants us to say yes. And you know what? That's not because he thinks we'll win."

"Let's vote," Rachel said. "Go."

"Go," Cassie agreed.

It was six out of six for going.

"Unanimous," Marco said.

I shook my head. "No. We're going to be seven. It's not unanimous till Erek votes."

"Go," a new voice said.

He appeared, standing in the middle of us. A normal-looking boy. Or that's what you'd think. The "boy" was a holographic projection. Inside the illusion was an android. An android who'd helped build the pyramids, who had taken on a hundred different human forms, letting each one seem to age, letting each one seem to die, then reappearing as some new holographic projection.

"You know what this is all about?" I asked Erek. Somewhere in the back of my mind I realized I had gotten used to the weirdness of people simply appearing out of nowhere. When the Ellimist was involved, things like that were normal.

"I know what it's about," Erek said with a nod.

His face was rigid, lips pressed tight together. It was impossible — I knew it was impossible — but still, I felt suppressed rage coming from the android. Barely contained violence.

"The Ellimist has brought me up to date,"

31

Erek confirmed. "If you'll have me, I'll go. I want to go. I . . . I have to go."

"You can't fight," Rachel said bluntly. "No offense, but I'd rather go get Jara Hamee or one of the other free Hork-Bajir. Or like Ax said, an Andalite warrior. We need firepower."

"Yes, but that won't be enough." Erek shook his head. "You won't defeat the Howlers in one-on-one combat. They are too deadly. You'll need more than your morphs. You'll have to outthink them. And I know them. I know the Howlers."

The argument hit home with Rachel. "Fair enough."

HAVE YOU CHOSEN? a huge voice asked.

I sighed. "Yeah, but can you give us a few days to —"

<Strangers! Strangers! Sell me your memories, strangers! Sell them to me, I beg of you.>

I was staring into a face not even a mother could love.

"Howler?" I asked shakily.

NO, ISKOORT, the Ellimist said. YOUR FAMILIES WILL NOT KNOW YOU HAVE GONE. BUT IF YOU DIE . . .

He let that hang. He didn't have to explain further.

"When does this fight start?" I cried, recoiling from the Iskoort face thrusting toward me.

IT HAS BEGUN.

CHAPTER 7

"Who invented this place, Dr. Seuss?" Marco demanded.

We were miles in the air. Miles from the ground, which we could see just over the edge of the platform. The platform with no railing, no warning. The platform that just stopped suddenly.

Below us was a twisting, leaning, propped-up-on-gigantic-support-beams structure of other platforms. Floors, I guess, all stuck here and there, sticking far out and not so far.

Above us was more of the same, till you'd swear the monstrous construction would reach the moon, assuming the Iskoort had a moon.

33

All of this was built of brilliantly colored blocks or bricks or segments.

Imagine that someone starts with all the Legos in the world. Add in all the Duplos and cheap bargain Duplos and let some humongous kid assemble them all into a tower a hundred miles tall.

Assume that no sensible adult ever becomes involved, except to come along occasionally and wedge in what looks like crutches the size of skyscrapers.

The floors could have been five feet apart, five hundred feet apart, or five miles apart. It was like no one figured it out till they built it.

I jumped back from the edge, feeling my stomach lurch and my heart stop. I had to push the Iskoort away to get safe, but I wasn't worried about politeness. I was trying not to take a fall that would last a couple of hours.

"Back up!" I yelled.

But now a whole gaggle of Iskoort were rushing us, honking with the diaphragm in their bellies and yammering in thought-speak, pushing us, shoving us by sheer mad exuberance toward the edge.

"Rachel!" Cassie cried.

I spun left just in time to see Rachel windmilling, her heels back over the edge of the platform.

"No!" I yelled as she lost the fight and top-pled backward.

I caught a blur of movement. When the blur stopped it was Erek, his hand holding Rachel by the arm as if she weighed no more than a candy bar.

Erek pulled her back up onto the platform.

"Did I mention I've always wanted you along on this mission, Erek?" Rachel said shakily. "Get back, you stupid jerks!"

This was directed at the press of a dozen Iskoort, all yammering incessantly.

<I will buy your memories!>

<Come visit my execution parlor!>

<Give me your clothing and I will give you credit!>

<Here! Eat this larva! Let it gestate and we'll split the proceeds between your heirs!>

<You stink horribly! I will cleanse you!>

And to Ax: <Become my partner and we will sell your fur as a *gachak* poison!>

"What is this, Planet of the Salesmen?" Marco demanded. "Back off! All of you, back off!"

"Man, I thought there were a lot of salespeo-ple at Nordstrom's, but this is nuts. I'll take care of this. I know how to get rid of pushy salespeo-ple." Rachel stepped out front, hands on her

35

hips. "We're just here to use the bathroom. Can you tell me where the ladies' room is?"

The Iskoort stared, goggle-eyed. Several of them wandered away. The others continued staring at us, waiting to see if we'd loosen up and do some business.

I looked at Cassie and we both sighed at the same time.

"Now what?" she wondered. "What do we do? Stand around till someone tries to kill us?"

I looked around, trying to get a grip on this bizarre place. There was no making sense of the structure itself. Our floor was a roomy one. At least a hundred feet separated our floor from the floor above. Back from the edge the small buildings began. They looked like clusters of igloos: blue and gold and white and green and red. Some were jumbled into piles several layers tall. Others were freestanding.

The Iskoort themselves came and went, in and out of the colored igloos, up and down the twisted, arched stairways connecting floors. They all looked busy. All in a hurry.

They were not the most frightening-looking race we'd ever encountered, but they were definitely not even slightly human.

They had heads like vultures, thrust forward on long necks. The necks protruded from shoulders that were a sort of oval platform, flat across.

From the shoulders dropped two arms, one on each side, each arm jointed three times, ending in a hand made up of one very long, tentacle-like finger, and two smaller, hooked, sharp-clawed fingers.

They walked in a way that made it seem they were crawling on their knees. Backward. Not that they went backward. They went forward. They had two thick legs, maybe two and a half feet long. Then came what looked like knees, followed by calves that extended forward, lying flat against the ground. Those ended in feet, each with a single long prehensile toe and two smaller claws jutting from the sides of thick pads.

Their midsection was bare of clothing and looked weirdly like an accordion — an accordion made of veined, pink flesh. It moved, wheezing out a sort of running commentary on their thought-speak.

It was the sound of a whine. A grating, annoying whine that rose or fell, depending, evidently, on how excited or mad or agitated they were.

"*The Nanny,*" Cassie observed.

"The what?"

"That sound. It sounds like Fran Drescher, the woman who plays the lead in *The Nanny.* No offense to her."

<I don't think Fran's probably around here to overhear you being rude,> Tobias pointed out.

Iskoort faces were, like I said, not attractive. They were roughly triangular with the point toward the top, which left no room for a pair of eyes to fit. So their eyes, pink as a rabbit's, were stuck on short stalks. They had mouths, but didn't use them to communicate. They pretty much stayed shut, opening only every few minutes to suck in air and reveal a fat, blue tongue and tiny, blue-tinged teeth.

Rachel said, "You know how you meet some people and right away, before they even say anything, before you have any idea what they're like, you don't like them? I mean, on sight you can't stand them? And it's not that they're ugly or anything, it's just something about them that sets you off?"

"No," Cassie said. "At least, I didn't know. Now I do."

A new assault team of Iskoort was quick-crawling toward us, heads thrust forward, eyes goggling.

<Forgive us, strangers!> the leader of this crowd said. <We did not expect off-worlders today. Welcome to the City of Beauty! Do you require a guide? Do you wish to sell your memories, or perhaps any unnecessary body parts?>

His diaphragm whined as he thought-spoke, a low, grating sound that rose and fell like a bagpipe blown by a man with too little wind.

I sighed. I was on the verge of suggesting that Rachel morph to grizzly bear and get rid of them, but Cassie said, "You know, if they're serious about a guide . . ."

"Yeah, you're right," I said, but I wasn't enthusiastic. "Um, well, we could use a guide. You know, to show us around. Show us where to stay."

<And what will you pay?> the Iskoort demanded, to the sound of eager whining.

"Well . . . we don't exactly have any money," I said.

<I will give you an excellent guide. My own grub! In exchange for her hair.>

He pointed one of his wormy tentacle fingers at Rachel. Or, more precisely, at her hair.

CHAPTER 8

The negotiation was not pretty.

The Iskoort wanted to shave Rachel's head. She explained very calmly that she would remove his head and use it for a soccer ball before that ever happened.

In the end, Rachel lost six inches of blond hair. What was left came to just below her ears.

"You know, it looks good," Cassie said.

"This from the girl who buys all her clothes from L.L. Bean," Rachel grumbled.

But the truth was, it did look good. Possibly because Erek did the cutting. "I used to cut Catherine the Great's hair," he explained, sounding apologetic, like it was embarrassing to admit that he'd been alive since Moses was wandering around in the desert.

In exchange, we got Guide. That was his name: Guide. His full name was Guide, Grub of Skin-seller, brother of Memory Wholesaler.

He was a young Iskoort. Which did not make him any less annoying. The first thing he did was try to improve the deal by getting Ax to let him have the last foot and a half of his tail.

Ax said no.

Marco said, "You know what? You jerk us around, Guide, and Ax *will* give you the last foot and a half of his tail."

Guide understood the threat. He became easier to deal with after that. He only asked for memories, clothing, hair, and various body parts every hour or so, rather than constantly.

"One question, right up front: Have you seen any other off-world strangers?" I asked him.

<Off-worlders? Of course! The City of Beauty is temporary home to many, many off-worlders.>

"Probably drawn here by the charm of the residents," Cassie said dryly.

It made me smile. I thought Cassie could like anyone. Evidently, even she had limits.

<We're looking for members of a species called Howlers,> Tobias said.

Guide's chest whined in a lower key. His

41

mouth gaped open. <This species is not known to me.>

I nodded and looked down at the bright red floor under my feet. "Don't lie to us, Guide. Have you ever met an Andalite before?"

Guide shot a nervous glance at Ax. <No.>

"Well, Andalites have the power to mind-meld with people. They can look right inside their thoughts and know if they're lying, and if you are lying, they make your head explode."

No one cracked a smile. Although Marco had to struggle.

<Now Ax is a Vulcan?> Tobias asked me in private thought-speak.

Guide's whine rose and fell. It probably meant something, but I didn't know what. Then, <Howlers? Did you say Howlers? There may be one or two Howlers around.>

"Try seven," I said. "Where are they? And do you know why they're here?"

<They come to trade, like all who visit our world. They trade memories for *boda* salts. Howler memories are very valuable.>

"What's this memory stuff?" Cassie asked. "You guys keep talking about buying memories. What's that all about?"

Guide looked surprised. I think. <You have never seen a memory show? Then that must be

our first stop! It is the greatest of entertainments!>

"Obviously, you don't get the Super Bowl here," Marco said.

"We always suspected the Howlers might have collective memory," Erek said. He surprised me. He'd been so quiet I'd practically forgotten he was with us. "The Howlers may pass memory along, generation to generation."

<Yes, yes,> Guide agreed. <This is why they command such a price. Their memories are long and very clear.>

I was feeling frustrated. We weren't getting anywhere. We'd just dropped in on this planet and so far we knew nothing. The Howlers could be watching us, ready to attack at any moment.

"Guide, have you seen these Howler memories?" Cassie asked him.

He laughed. <No. Not me. I am a Trader, a probationary member of the Guild of Traders. I am not interested in violence and killing and slaughter. No, it is the members of the Criminal Guild and the Warmaker Guild who buy Howler memories.>

I was getting that nervous, jumpy feeling I get when I feel like I'm being delayed from doing something vital. I felt we were wasting our time talking to the Iskoort.

"We aren't here to write a paper on the Iskoort," I said, more rudely than I'd intended. "We're here to take down the seven Howlers so we can go home."

Cassie looked a little hurt. But in a very calm voice she said, "It just seemed to me that if we have to have a battle, we'd be better off if we knew where we were and what was going on."

She was right, of course. But the edginess I felt wouldn't let me admit it. "We need a place. A base of operations. We can't just stand out here in the open."

<Then come, follow me!> Guide said. <I know the right place.>

He started off, moving in his weird backward crawling way, whining from his chest the whole way. We went down a set of steps, something the Iskoort did literally backward, but with surprising agility and speed.

We came out on a new level, mostly dark blue, and utterly different from the previous level. Here we saw none of the igloos, only a vast field of small cylinders, maybe two feet tall.

<Energy storage,> Guide explained, and led us down another stairway, this one much longer. We stuck rigidly to the center of the stairs — from the top it was perhaps a half-mile drop to the mustard-colored floor below. Only Tobias was

comfortable, flying around and beneath the stairway.

I suppose Erek felt safe enough, too. It was hard to imagine the android ever missing a step. This level, this mustard-yellow level, was teeming with Iskoort, moving slowly along narrow avenues between open-front buildings.

It was easy to recognize what this level was.

"It's the mall," Rachel said. "A bazaar."

<Yes, this is the level seventy-eight marketplace,> Guide confirmed. <We must move quickly here.>

"What? No shopping?" Rachel, of course.

We reached the floor and were instantly surrounded by jabbering, poking, pushing, whining Iskoort, all desperate to buy whatever we had and sell us whatever we didn't.

"I see what you mean by moving quickly, Guide," I said.

<What? No, no, not for these honest Traders. But this market is a favorite gathering place for members of the Warmaker Guild.>

I had about three seconds to think *what?* before something slammed me violently to the floor.

45

CHAPTER 9

I was down, flat on my back, a weight on my chest. A bony head, stubby horns protruding from the top, was just above mine.

"Howlers!" I yelled.

I twisted and tried to roll away. But the bony-headed creature wouldn't let me go. He slammed his head down at me. I jerked my head to the side, hard. The blunt horns struck the floor.

I did something I haven't had to do much, despite being in more battles than I can remember: I drew back my fist and punched.

I caught the Howler in his gaping mouth. He jerked back. I drew my legs up, thighs against my chest, and I kicked.

Thump!

I caught the Howler flat in his chest diaphragm. He fell back, flailing but unbalanced. I was up in a flash.

My friends were all under attack. No one had had time to morph. Tobias was ripping at the short stalk eyes of a Howler. I saw Ax snap his tail and remove an arm that had been around Cassie's throat.

Rachel kicked another in a place that humans don't like to have kicked. One of the Howlers was flailing away at Erek, head-butting him and having no effect as Erek stood there calmly.

Rachel was halfway into her grizzly bear morph and already growling with a voice that was still mostly her own.

Something was not right. Not right at all. We weren't even morphed and we were beating these guys. And Erek was way too calm. Then it occurred to me. I had kicked my guy in his diaphragm. His whining, Iskoort diaphragm.

"Erek! Are these Howlers?"

"No. Of course not," he said calmly.

Our assailants backed up. There were five of them. One looked bleakly at the stub of his arm. The others gaped at us and whined through their chests.

They were Iskoort. Not like Guide, at least not exactly. The bodies were mostly the same, but the heads and hands were different. Their heads

47

were wider at the top, with the two little nubs of horn. Their hands were less delicate, the claws larger than the tentacle. Their legs were flexed, not as flat, allowing them to move faster, in leaps, not crawls.

<These are Iskoort of the Warmaker Guild,> Guide said, like he was introducing a bunch of guys from a different school. <This is why we must hurry. They don't like off-worlders.>

<They're going to like us a lot less if they try that again!> Rachel said.

"Let's get out of here," I said. "Rachel? Stay in morph. Ax, you stay ready, too. That should be enough to handle these guys."

We were attacked twice more by two different gangs of Warmaker Iskoort before we could reach the next stairway. They were easy enough to deal with, but I still managed to get bruised up. And by the time we were safely out of the market-place, Rachel said what we were all starting to feel.

"Just tell me this: Why, exactly, does the El-limist want to save these guys? I'm starting to think maybe Crayak is on the right track."

We headed down the stairway, finally starting to laugh at the bizarre experience with the War-maker Iskoort. Feeling relaxed and a little cocky after so easily beating the local tough guys.

The stairway we were on was wider, though still without rails, but we were getting used to that. It was wider to make room for two-way traffic, and several Iskoort, many like Guide, but others subtly different, passed us by.

The next level was maybe two hundred feet down. Guide was out front. I was laughing at some joke Marco made.

"Howler!" Erek yelled.

"Yeah, right," Marco said. But he looked. And I looked.

"Erek," I said as calmly as I could, "are you joking?"

His projected face was white. I wondered how much of projecting an emotion was automatic with him after so long as a human.

"I am not joking, Jake," he said. "That is a Howler."

CHAPTER 10

The Howler was moving up the stairway. We were moving down. We froze. The Howler kept coming.

He was not huge. Smaller than a Hork-Bajir. As big as a large man. He walked on two bowed legs with a swinging, almost comic gait. He had two arms, longer than his legs. The hands were almost human, five fingers and an opposable thumb. But from the wrists projected a sort of second hand, a claw that could be lowered to cover the back of the hand, or kept up out of the way. This claw had four hooked, steel-tipped claws.

It looked like there was a bearing halfway up

his body, as if the top half of the torso was on a living lazy Susan, allowing the body to turn all the way around and keep the fighting claws in the game.

The head was ugly, a slag heap of melted-looking, black pebbled skin. The entire creature looked like he had been formed out of still-cooling lava. Beneath the black, in the cracks and creases of his flesh, were lines of bright red.

Within this face were eyes of a startlingly beautiful blue. Robin's egg blue, they call it. The entire eye was blue, with the cat's iris a paler shade.

The Howler seemed indifferent to us. Didn't care. Wasn't concerned.

He wore a series of loose belts around his torso, and each of these featured a different weapon. Or at least they looked like weapons. Something similar to a Dracon beam, what might almost have been an automatic pistol, knives, small metallic boomerangs, a gun that seemed loaded with darts.

He was a walking arsenal.

I looked back at Erek, above me on the stairs. His face was flickering. In and out. Not with emotion. With simple loss of control. The android under the hologram kept peeking out.

The Howler's empty blue eyes locked on Erek.

"Erek, get a grip," I said with forced calm.

He shook himself and the hologram stabilized, but the Howler kept watching him.

"Six against one, Jake," Rachel said. "We won't get better odds."

I felt my stomach clench. Sheer drop on both sides. Unknown terrain below. Not the *place* for a fight. But Rachel was right: It was the *time*.

"Morph," I said quietly. "Ax? You take the lead. Tobias? Get some altitude. Guide? Back off, this isn't your fight. Erek? Stay out of the way."

That sounded harsher than I'd intended. But my heart was hammering and I was feeling the fear-sweat down my back. It had happened too soon. We weren't ready. We were tired from the run-ins with the Warmaker Iskoort.

But mostly, mostly I was seeing pictures in my head. The eye. Crayak. The image from my dream. I could almost hear him laughing. Just a figment of my imagination, but it felt real enough.

Six against one. It wasn't going to get any better.

I began to morph, to call on the tiger DNA that swam through my blood. The tiger would be bigger than the Howler. *The six of us together in morph can take on anything,* I told myself. We can take on anything.

The Howler's blue eyes narrowed as we shifted positions. He knew a fight when he saw one coming. But he was fascinated by the morphing. Fascinated and almost jealous, if it's possible to read an expression on a face made of tar with eyes as empty as sky.

I felt the morph working on my body. The orange fur grew from my hands and arms. I had no time to get out of my clothes. They'd be torn apart by the morphing. Fur spread across my body. My fingers swelled, dark leather on the palms, orange and white on the back. Claws that could leave slash marks in a car door grew to replace my useless human fingernails.

I heard the organs inside me shifting, squishing, relocating, configuring themselves for the tiger body.

A long tail sprouted from the base of my spine and immediately began to snap back and forth, twitching in agitation and anticipation.

I fell forward onto all fours. This made my head several steps lower than my hindquarters. Teeth filled my mouth, too big, so big they grew out like a saber-toothed cat's teeth.

Then my mouth caught up and my face grew sensitive whiskers. My eyes, made for seeing through darkness like it was day. My nose, sensitive to every smell of animal life. My ears, pricked forward, quivering at attention.

The Howler looked a little less intimidating now. The tiger was not worried. The tiger knew it was the fastest, deadliest creature in the jungle. The tiger did not fear the strange-smelling creature.

Ax was just in front of me, tail bowed and ready, three eyes forward, the remaining stalk eye watching the rest of us. Rachel had morphed to grizzly bear. She stood up, a massive pillar of rough brown fur with power to uproot small trees. Marco had morphed to gorilla. He swung his pile driver arms back and forth almost casually, like he was waiting on the street corner for the bus to come. Cassie had morphed to wolf. The thick armor of fur on the back of her neck stood on end, and she'd drawn back her muzzle, revealing wet, glistening teeth.

We were more than a ton of muscle and claw and tooth, all directed by human intelligence that could draw on animal instinct.

Facing us, a single, man-sized alien.

I realized Erek was talking. That he had been for several seconds and I'd been too distracted to hear him.

". . . will paralyze you and numb your senses. If he gets close he'll use the needle teeth retracted into his upper and lower jaw. He's not as fast as —"

<Erek. What did you say about paralyzing?> I interrupted.

"It's the reason they're called Howlers, Jake. The voice. Be ready to —"

The Howler's hand moved. Reaching for the beam weapon!

CHAPTER 11

"Hhhhhrrroooowwwwrrrr!" I roared, a sound that made brave men fall down trembling.

I gathered myself for a leap. But Ax was faster. His tail snapped, crack!

The Howler's hand dropped. The weapon clattered down the stairs. But before the weapon had stopped rolling, the hand was growing back!

<Attack!> I yelled.

I leaped. Ax whipped his tail again, faster than the eye could follow.

I roared again, bellowing a sound that had never been heard on planet Iskoort. The others surged behind me. Down we went, a ton of animal power.

Then the Howler replied.

"KEEEEEEEEEEEEEEE-row."

It was a blast of sound like nothing I'd ever heard before. Compared to it, my tiger's roar was the mewling of a kitten.

"KEEEEEEEEEEEEEEE-row."

I missed my leap and fell in a tangle on the steps. I saw Rachel trip and fall, landing on top of me. It was like having a safe dropped on my stomach.

The wind exploded from my lungs. I scrambled to get up, but I couldn't make sense of up or down. I clawed feebly. Rachel rolled off and I saw that Ax was reeling, running! Running away, back up the stairs, weak Andalite hands clapped against his ears, blood seeping between the fingers.

Cassie was howling, all wolf in her pain.

Marco seemed the least affected. He swung a cement-block fist that hit the Howler on his arm and spun the creature sideways.

I got to my feet, hoping to attack while the Howler was off-balance. Except the Howler wasn't off-balance. The ball-bearing waist twirled him all the way around, using the force of Marco's blow to spin and bring the now-regenerated hand up to a weapon.

F-t-t-t-t-t-t!

He had fired! A dozen steel darts, tiny triangles, ripped a messy hole through my left front leg. I stumbled. The pain was intense.

Marco swung another fist, missed! The Howler turned the flechette gun on him. A bloody hole you could have pushed a Coke can through appeared in Marco's back.

He dropped like a load of bricks.

Cassie had recovered enough to bound into action, using Marco's fallen mass as a springboard. The Howler raised the gun, but too slowly. Wolf jaws clamped down on the arm and Cassie held on like a bulldog, ripping, tearing.

I was up and moving on three legs. A lame leap! I clamped my teeth on Howler leg. Rachel was up, too, and charging on all fours, looking to knock the creature down.

Tobias came swooping down at full-stoop speed, talons out for the Howler's eyes. We were getting the upper hand!

"KEEEEEEEEEE-row!"

Someone exploded a hand grenade in my head. I clamped my jaws tight, but all else was a blur, a swirling, mad blur.

Blue-and-tan fur leaped over me, rust-red feathers shot past. What? What was happening? I couldn't think . . . couldn't make sense . . .

A searing sharp pain. My eyes cleared just

long enough to see the ornate dagger handle that protruded from my neck.

I'd been stabbed! In the neck. The tiger's blood . . . my blood . . .

"Jake! Demorph!" Erek said in a voice loud enough to penetrate the death fog creeping through my brain.

Then there came other orders, all rapped out in a loud, clear voice. No, not orders. Just information.

"Cassie, he's trying to stab you. Ax, you are too close to the edge, stop moving! Rachel, the Howler is within two feet of the edge, to your right."

I was demorphing. Or at least I thought I was. I couldn't be sure. The tiger was dying, blood pumping out of his severed neck arteries. "Demorph, Jake! Demorph!" Erek's loud voice urged. "Do it now!"

I heard a bear's roar. I heard an impact: body against body. I saw nothing but shapes, meaningless shapes.

"Cassie, demorph!" Erek ordered. "He's gutted you, demorph! Do it now."

From far off, a hawk's cry. A bear's bellow. The bullwhip crack of an Andalite tail.

All far, far away.

59

CHAPTER 12

Crayak turned his bloodred eye on me, watching as I lay helpless. Watching as the Howlers stood around Cassie in a circle, watching as they lowered their claw hands into place, watching and laughing as she stood, eyes closed, helpless, seconds away from —

"Cassie! Look out!"

I jerked up, eyes wide, hands flailing, fending off an attack.

"Chill, chill," Marco said. He grabbed one hand and Rachel grabbed the other. "It's okay, dude, fight's over."

I looked around, still wild. A room. Walls of solid colors, one red, the others yellow. Still in Lego Land.

I slapped my legs. Human. My arms. Human. All me, with no ragged holes.

I'd made it out of morph. I looked around the room. Rachel and Marco. Tobias sitting on the back of a strangely shaped chair. Erek standing alone, head down in thought. Ax as far from me as he could get, all four eyes turned away.

"Cassie?" I asked.

"I'm here," she said. I realized she was behind me. I felt her palm on my cheek. Then she put her arms around me and hugged me from behind. It made me want to cry.

"It's taken you a while to wake up," Cassie said. "You barely demorphed in time. Then it was like you were in a coma, like you weren't going to wake up at all."

I remembered dreams. They were dreams, weren't they? Hard to be sure. Reality itself was weird enough to be a dream.

"The Howler?" I asked Rachel.

Her mouth was an angry line. "We hurt him. But he walked away."

"Six against one and we got a draw," Marco said angrily.

"Not six," Rachel corrected. "Seven. Erek saved our butts. He was the only one who could handle the howls."

"Yeah, right, thanks a huge load, Erek," Marco said angrily. "He gave us directions. Not to hurt the Howler, you understand, 'cause that would violate his programming. But directions on how to crawl out of there."

I held on to Cassie's hand. I didn't want to get into this. I wanted to hold on to a moment of feeling glad to be alive, glad to feel Cassie's concern.

Then I sighed, squeezed her fingers, and pushed her hand away. "Erek did what he could, Marco. You know that as well as I do. My brain was scrambled. I'd be dead without him. That's enough for me."

Marco looked like he wanted to say something else, but then his anger collapsed. "Yeah. We all did what we could."

I spotted Guide back against a wall, uncharacteristically quiet. "You stick with us after that?" I asked him.

His eyes glowed. <Oh, yes, yes, yes. I will be able to sell the memory of that battle for a small fortune! And if each of you would sell me your own unique perspectives, I could buy my own corner with the profits!>

I drew Cassie around to where I could see her. I nodded at Ax. "What's with him?" I asked.

She shook her head. "He ran away. He came back, but I guess that's not enough. He won't talk to anyone."

"Let him be for a while," I said. "Then I'll talk to him."

I felt weary. Bruised and beaten, although my human body reconstructed from DNA was unscarred by the battle. It was my brain that was worn out. I could see similar feelings on the faces around me.

We'd been beaten in a fair fight. No, not a *fair* fight. It had been six of us plus Erek against one Howler. We'd fought to a draw. A tie. Seven against one. A tie.

If there had been two Howlers, let alone all seven, we'd have been killed in ten seconds.

We weren't scared, not the way we might be, facing a battle. We were worse than scared: We were beaten.

"What is this place?" I asked.

Rachel shrugged. "Some place Guide got for us. This room and a bathroom — well, I think it's a bathroom. Hope it's a bathroom."

A pile of rags lay in one corner. Our clothing. What was left of it after we'd morphed while still wearing it. We were in our morphing outfits now. But I guessed we didn't look any more out of place than we would have, anyway. The Iskoort probably didn't care much about human fashion.

<What do we do?> Tobias asked.

"I'm for dialing up the Ellimist and telling

him to go jump off whatever super-dimensional bridge he can find," Marco said.

<He wouldn't have put us here if we weren't at least theoretically capable of winning,> Tobias said.

"Unless there's some other, deeper game the Ellimist is playing," Cassie said. "He's fighting a battle for entire species, entire planets. We're just pawns."

That was more cynicism than I was used to hearing from Cassie. But she wasn't wrong. The Ellimist and Crayak were both way over our heads. And I was haunted by the suggestion that maybe this was all a setup. That maybe Crayak wanted us here. Not because we were important by ourselves, but because eliminating us would help the Yeerks.

Why had the Ellimist brought us here? He had to know how powerful the Howlers were. Had to.

"This is a rotten, stinking deal," Rachel said, expressing the thoughts in my own head. "We're leaving our own planet defenseless to save these Iskoort." She said "Iskoort" like a curse word.

I found myself looking at Erek. I could only imagine what was going on inside his head. He had the power to fight Howlers and win. But wasn't able to fight.

Erek said, "Maybe the Ellimist would reprogram me. Remove the prohibition against violence."

Marco groaned. "Well, it's official: The situation is hopeless. When Erek starts talking that way it's because we're beat."

"Beat *this*," Rachel said rudely.

It made me smile. Rachel felt as down as anyone, but she refused to admit she couldn't just go out and nail the next Howler she saw.

"They're faster than we are, stronger than we are, better armed than we are," Cassie said glumly. Then she lifted her face, eyes wary. "But are they smarter than we are?"

"Erek?" I asked him.

He sighed, a very human reaction. "They had faster-than-light ships at a time when humans still thought the wheel was a radical new invention."

<Doesn't make them smarter,> Tobias said. <The Ellimist said some species evolve quickly, others slowly. If you get a billion years' head start, of course you have better weapons and technology than a species that started later. Doesn't mean you're smarter. Maybe it just means you started earlier.>

It was a weak thread to hang by. But it was all we had.

"Erek? Tell us all you know about the Howlers," I said.

65

CHAPTER 13

"I only saw them from the point of view of the victims," Erek said. "I can use my holographic systems to recreate what I saw. But there may be a way to get even more information."

<Yes!> Guide said, picking up on it right away. <Yes, of course. You could purchase Howler memories!> He walked over to the wall and touched a panel. The panel opened. A shelf popped out, an array of buttons and colored touch pads.

<I can load memories directly into your android friend, here. But they will be expensive.>

"You're not getting any more of my hair," Rachel warned. "Not a kidney or an arm, either."

Guide whined from the diaphragm in his

chest. It may have been a laugh of some kind. <I will pay for you to view the Howler memories. In exchange for harvesting your own memories.>

I sucked in a breath. "What is this memory-selling? Does it mean we lose our memories?"

Guide looked perplexed. <Of course not. Why would it? We simply make a copy.>

"They Xerox our memories?"

<Can't do it,> Tobias said. <Those memories could end up reaching the Yeerks.>

He was right. Maybe. "Ax?"

No answer. Ax was swaying slightly, back and forth. His tail was low, curved forward. He was way deep in private thoughts.

"Ax!" I said louder. "Ax, we need you."

He looked up, startled. <Yes, Prince Jake.>

I didn't tell him not to call me Prince. This wasn't going to be handled with a little joshing. The Andalites are an essentially peaceful race, but with a long warrior tradition, too. Ax was an *aristh*. A military cadet. And he'd spent his entire life in the shadow of his brother, Elfangor, who was considered a great war hero.

"How far are we from the closest Yeerk outpost?" I asked him.

<I . . . I don't know where we are. I don't have a star chart.>

Guide touched a wall panel. A small, flat

67

screen appeared. Muttering and whining to himself, Guide called up a star chart. It was meaningless to me, of course.

Ax looked at it with no visible interest. He touched the screen, pulling the perspective back, widening the view. He did this twice more, till even I could recognize the spiral arms of our own Milky Way galaxy.

<We are more than five hundred million light years from Earth,> Ax said. <Before the Yeerks could spread a tenth of this distance they would have had to swallow not only Earth, but my planet as well.>

I nodded. "Thanks. Okay, then. It's a deal, Guide. But if I understand what you've told me, our memories would make you very, very rich. So this is it. If we live, you get to copy our memories. And you don't ask for anything else, and you advance us whatever we need."

I thought Guide was going to fall over. I had the feeling we'd just turned him into the Bill Gates of the Iskoort.

<I will transfer all archived Howler memories to the android.>

"The android has a name: Erek," Rachel snapped.

<He can call himself the Grand Guildmaster as far as I am concerned!> Guide said happily.

Guide tapped into the panel. Then he called

Erek over. He pointed to a slot like a keyhole. <Can you interface?>

Erek dropped his hologram, revealing his true android body. From one steel finger a prong telescoped out and pressed into the keyhole. The steel finger changed shape to conform to the keyhole shape.

Erek's almost canine face was blank. Then his eyes flew open and he pulled back. It was impossible to read emotion on the android face. But I could guess. He had just absorbed the memories of the creatures who had wiped out his creators, the Pemalites, and made interstellar fugitives of the Chee.

"How are you doing, Erek?" Cassie asked.

"I have absorbed the available Howler memories. They are not . . . not pleasant viewing."

"Can you show us?"

"Yes." He hesitated. "Memories of the attack on my creators is included. I would not like to show you that. I would not like to have to . . ." He fell silent, embarrassed.

Cassie put a hand on his steel and ivory arm. "Then don't. Show us what you can. Show us what we need to know."

Erek nodded. "The planet I'll show you has no name. The people call themselves Graffen's Children. What I will show you happened approximately twenty Earth years ago."

The bare room disappeared as Erek's hologram filled the room with a forest in shades of purple, blue-green, and mustard-yellow. We saw enormous leaves, as big as bedsheets. Vines wound along the ground, dipped in and out of the dark soil, then shot up to form strange trees.

Birds in long, random shapes like pink feather boas swooped and wove through the leaves and branches. Below them, orange-and-yellow centipedes crept along. Bristly combs rose from their backs, making them look like a comic cross between worms and stegosauruses. Animals like two-headed prairie dogs popped up out of subterranean lairs, spit out mouthfuls of dirt and disappeared again.

It was a rain forest. But someone else's. With wonders no more magical than those of Earth, but wonders just the same.

Through the forest came a column of creatures that made me laugh. "Gumby," I said.

They looked like Gumby. Not green, but dark blue, and not smooth, but as rough-textured as an old tree. But still they moved with the jerky grace of Gumby, walking on two legs, eyes raised to the treetops above them.

I saw a hand move into view and I jerked in surprise. A Howler's hand! I was seeing this forest, these plants and animals and Graffen's Children, through Howler eyes.

70

The Howler was lying in wait, hidden from view.

Then the nearest of the Graffen's Children spotted him. His eyes went wide. A smile twisted his strange mouth. He extended a hand toward the Howler, welcoming, curious.

The column of Graffen's Children walked toward the Howler like so many toddlers. Like kids who wanted to pet a dog or something.

The Howler moved, a blur of speed. Other Howlers came into view. They howled. To us the sound was softened by Erek's filtering. But it hit the Graffen's Children full force. They began to blow apart. They stood there, helpless, confused, not knowing why anyone would hurt them, and they simply —

"Erek, stop it!" I snapped.

The hologram disappeared as quickly as a TV picture that had been turned off.

"I shouldn't have let you do this, Erek. Can you erase this stuff from your memory?"

"No, Jake."

"I'm sorry," I said. "How much more did you absorb?"

Erek powered up his human hologram. His face was human again. Now I could see the emotions Erek was feeling. "I have memories of seventeen Howler attacks. All successful. They have never been defeated. They have attacked

71

highly advanced civilizations and simple people like Graffen's Children. They have never taken a prisoner. They simply kill and kill and kill until there is no one left to kill. Then they go and find something else to kill."

"That's insane!" Cassie yelled. "No species does that. It doesn't make sense. There's no logic to it. You're not talking about predators who kill to eat, or prey animals who kill in self-defense. Even humans have reasons, no matter how sick. Even humans have limits. Why would evolution result in a species that kills for no reason?"

"It wouldn't. It didn't," Erek said. "The Howlers didn't evolve. They were created."

"Crayak?"

He nodded. "Graffen's Children and dozens of species were annihilated by Crayak's Children."

CHAPTER 14

We slept in shifts. Two of us on guard at all times. A futile gesture. If the Howlers found us, we would die.

Guide assured us we were safe. Apartments were built strong enough to resist the often rambunctious Warmaker Iskoort. And with our bargain to give him our memories, I felt like he had an interest in keeping us alive.

But so far, the Iskoort generally didn't impress me. I was sure that others, with less at stake, would sell us out.

It was a long night. It was a very long night. Maybe some of us slept. I didn't. I didn't want to dream.

I tried to make sense of it all. Tried to figure

73

out what the Ellimist thought he was doing. How he expected us to win a fight we had no hope of winning.

But nothing made sense. Whatever game the Ellimist was playing was over our heads. I felt like an ant wandering around a chessboard, trying to figure out the rules when all I could see was colossal figures moving around me in inexplicable patterns.

All we had learned was that the Howlers were violent beyond belief. Destructive. That they were, in fact, designed and built to be pure evil.

"What's it like to be one of them?" Cassie whispered in the darkness. She was close by. Obviously not sleeping, either.

"Who? An Iskoort?"

"No. A Howler. They know they were created by Crayak. They're bright enough to fly spacecraft, so they can't be entirely without minds. What do they think of themselves?"

I didn't really care. But Cassie's voice was a comforting distraction. "I don't know. I guess they're happy being what they are. Aren't most species happy being themselves?"

Long silence, as she considered that. "Maybe I would have believed that back in the old days. But you know, I've been a termite, an ant. Mindless creatures of instinct. They weren't happy. Not unhappy, either. They just do what they're programmed to do, and they don't have minds, really, so what else can they do? But Howlers must have minds."

"Just because a person or whatever is intelligent, that doesn't mean they can't be brutal and rotten and evil. I mean, there must have been some smart Nazis and some smart slave owners."

"Yeah, but the Howlers aren't just individuals. We're talking about an entire species, an entire race, being evil. That isn't possible. We know that. Even the Yeerks aren't all one way."

"And maybe the Howlers are. All one way, I mean. Maybe you just have a race that is pure evil."

"Can't be," Cassie said confidently.

"Why not?"

"Because that's what Nazis and slave owners and people like that believed. That you can just take a whole race or whatever and say 'they're all this or all that.' That's never going to be true."

"Maybe," I said, not wanting to stomp on her idealism. "Maybe so. But what are the odds that these seven Howlers handpicked by Crayak are going to be all soft and cuddly?"

She fell silent. So I guess I'd stomped on her idealism, anyway. At some level I thought, *Good. We don't need a bunch of happy talk when we're up against Howlers.* But at another level I was just mad at the world and confused and scared.

I started to say "Cassie . . ." when something hit the door with the impact of a small comet.

WHAM!

We were up and awake in a billionth of a second.

WHAM!

The door held, amazingly. Guide started to whine. <See! I told you —>

TSEEEEEEW!

A red circle appeared in the door and began to smoke and burn.

"It's them!" I yelled. "Howlers!"

I felt like I was choking on my own heart, like it was beating so hard, so fast, that it filled me up, leaving no room for any but small, gasping breaths.

We were going to die!

I heard moans of terror. Some were coming from me, just these subhuman, animal moans of fear.

"Morph!" I yelled, choking out the word.

"They're going to kill us!" Marco cried.

In the glow of the Dracon beam, I saw Ax walking steadily toward the door. Rough, shaggy hair was sprouting from Rachel's face.

"NO!" I blurted, realizing the mistake. "Not combat morphs! Go small! Flies!"

I tried to focus my jangled, shattered-glass brain on the image of a fly. It was the only way out. Not to fight, but to run.

<I will attempt to slow them down,> Ax said calmly.

"No, Ax. Morph! We have to get out of here!" Rachel yelled at him.

<I ran once,> Ax said. <Not again.>

<Not the time, Ax-man!> Tobias said.

<I am an Andalite warrior!> he said harshly.

TSEEEEEEEEW!

The beam suddenly burned through into the room and hit the far wall.

Erek ran to the hole in the door as a Howler stuck his head though, eyes greedy. Erek's hologram was gone. He was now a Chee.

"Chee!" the Howler said in surprise.

Erek took one steel hand and calmly rammed his fingers into the metal of the door. They went through like he was sticking his hand in a loaf of bread. He did the same with the other hand, curling his fingers and gripping the handholds he had created.

He blocked the entrance with his body. The Howler sneered and shoved at him. Erek did not move by so much as an atom's width.

The Howler backed up and leveled his flechette gun at Erek's metallic face. He fired. Flechettes ricocheted around the room, but Erek was unharmed.

"Jake, this will not last," Erek warned me.

We were all morphing at top speed. All but

77

Ax. I already had huge, bulging fly eyes and six legs.

<Ax! Do it! Morph, right now!>

<No, I can't run again!>

<Aximili-Esgarrouth-Isthill, you call me "prince" and you act like you mean it and I am giving you a direct order. Morph. Do. It. NOW!>

CHAPTER 15

Now the Howlers tried their ultimate weapon. The howl was earsplitting. The walls around Erek began to shiver and crack. Guide fell to the ground, rolling in agony.

Ax's eyes were bleeding, even in midmorph. But the rest of us were more fly than human, and the waves of vibration from the Howlers did not cause us pain. Not pain, just an overwhelming instinct to fly. Vibration could be sound or it could be movement. The fly brains felt the howl as sudden, massive, threatening movements from every direction at once.

Still seven or eight pounds, with a twisting, morphing human mouth, I was beating my

79

growing wings frantically, kicking in panic, trying to fly.

"Fight me, Chee," the Howler taunted, when he realized his howl would not shake Erek's grip.

I was shocked to recognize the language. He was speaking English! Crayak must have programmed it into this bunch of Howlers. Programmed them to understand our language and to be able to taunt and question us, if necessary.

Erek ignored him. The Howlers began to fire Dracon beams. Not at Erek. They must have known from their collective memory that Chee cannot be easily destroyed by beam weapons.

Instead, they were using the Dracon beams to slice around Erek's handholds.

We had all morphed. All panicked, but all morphed. Except Ax, who was still partly Andalite. And Guide, who was sitting in a corner now, gazing raptly at the madness, creating valuable memories for later sale.

Suddenly, Erek's handhold was gone, burned away. The Howlers pushed past him, contemptuous. They knew he could not fight. But they found nothing. Nothing that looked like the creatures one of them had fought on the stairs.

Nothing except a weak, defenseless Ax, still morphing. A hideously misshapen, melting, twisting monstrosity.

The Howlers piled into the room. With my compound eyes they seemed to be made of glowing purple and blue with pulsating black veins. The facets in my fun-house-mirror eyes broke them into pieces. They were everywhere around me as I flew unnoticed.

"Target?" one Howler asked another. This second Howler was slightly larger and carrying even more weapons.

"Yes. Kill it!" the leader bellowed in rage.

Seven flechette guns rose and took aim at Ax. He had no chance. None.

Erek leaped to put himself between the guns and Ax, but the Howlers calmly blocked his path. And Erek's programming would not allow him to shove them aside.

In a split second, Ax would be annihilated.

<Crayak is a huge, walking, talking pimple,> a thought-speak voice said.

Marco!

The Howlers' heads snapped around, left, right, their bodies swiveling as they searched for the one who taunted them. They aimed at Guide, who was crawling out through the hole they'd burned.

<Not me! Not me! I'm just an Iskoort trader! And by the way, I'd love to buy your memories of all this!>

<And Howlers are the cowards of the galaxy. Brainless, ugly, bad-smelling, sniveling, gutless worms,> Marco added.

"Forget it," the leader ordered. "Voices are meaningless."

I zipped through the air, flying in the wild, wobbly fly way. I aimed for the face of the Howler leader. I landed just beneath his left eye.

<Not just a voice, you walking dirtball. I'm right here. Think you're tough? Try killing me.>

The hand snapped up with shocking speed. I felt it coming, felt the disturbances in the air, and I responded with the RIGHT NOW speed of the fly.

Alien fingers slapped toward me. I fired my wings. The Howler was so fast his fingers missed me by millimeters.

<How are you going to kill us?> Marco taunted. <Better go back to Crayak and explain that you've failed.>

"Forget them! Kill that —"

<Too late,> Ax said.

Ax had made the transition to fly.

<Okay, stay airborne. No one land, no one set down,> I said. I was beginning to feel just the smallest bit of optimism. Even relief. The Howlers were mystified.

"The android!" the Howler leader roared.

I looked. I could see Erek, or at least a shimmering, distorted version of him. But the Howlers no longer could. Erek had created a hologram of one of the walls. He was standing calmly behind it. Out of sight, though not out of reach.

<Let's bail before these guys start thinking of ways to swat flies,> Cassie suggested.

<You got that right,> Marco agreed.

<Out the door,> I said. <But stay close.>

We zipped, unnoticed, through the burned-out doorway.

Not a victory. All we had managed to do was run away. But we were all still alive. And that was more than I would have thought possible.

Too bad just staying alive was not an option. We had to win. We had to destroy seven creatures, any one of whom could fight all of us to a draw.

<Guide. Can you hear me?>

<Yes, of course. I am not far away.>

CHAPTER 16

<We know,> Rachel said. <We're just above your head. No, don't look!>

<They'll watch Guide,> Tobias said. <If we hook up with him and demorph, they'll have us.>

The seven Howlers had emerged from the wrecked apartment. We'd lost track of them after that. Fly eyes are useless at any distance beyond a foot or two. Were they tracking us? Or Guide? No way to know. But you couldn't get careless with Howlers.

<Erek. I know you can't answer, but if you can hear me, try to find Guide. Hide him from the Howlers.>

As we watched Guide, another "Iskoort" sidled up next to him. The second Iskoort suddenly became a small group of Warmaker Iskoort who simply absorbed Guide.

This group of Warmaker Iskoort would have been revealed as a hologram if anyone had touched them. But no one did.

We flew into the hologram and landed on Erek's head.

<Are we clear?> I asked Erek.

"We were being watched, but I believe we have lost the Howlers, at least for now."

<Great,> Rachel said unenthusiastically. <We can stay alive as long as we're flies hiding inside a hologram.>

<I will take you to a new place where you can hide,> Guide said. <Incidentally, this ability you have to change shapes is very interesting. Is it perhaps a technology you can sell? I would pay top price.>

I didn't bother answering. We demorphed back to human and hawk and Andalite, still hidden, bunched up within the hologram.

We were crossing a sort of large square or plaza. The floor was green in this area and almost made you think you were on a vast lawn. In the center of the square was yet another stairway, and we took it, heading down. It was busy, with lots of Iskoort coming and

85

going and what I assumed to be a few aliens, as well.

Erek made the hologram growl and threaten repeatedly, to keep anyone from bumping into us and penetrating our illusion.

We came at last to the next level down. And this was definitely different. Instead of the bare openness of previous levels, this one was almost a jungle. But a unique one. The plants, trees, and flowers were all in planter boxes packed together, leaving only narrow, circuitous walkways. If you looked out and up, you'd think you were in a genuine jungle. If you looked down, you felt more like you were walking through a greenhouse.

Iskoort were packed in tight on the walkways. Too tight for our extended hologram.

"Tobias," I said. "Think you could get up and see if we're being followed?"

Tobias flew out of the top of the hologram, took a couple of turns, and came back. <Looks clear.>

"I can't imagine the Howlers creeping along like spies, anyway," Rachel said. "They're a little more direct. If they see us, they'll come after us, and too bad for anyone who gets in the way."

Erek turned off the extended hologram and resumed his human appearance. We were exposed again. Aliens walking in what passed for a park. My skin tingled.

86

"Ax, keep an eye out in all directions," I said. He was the only one of us who could look backward as easily as forward.

"Yeah, let us know if you see any Howlers so we can have a few seconds to cry before they get us," Marco said darkly.

Through the maze of false forest, we shuffled along with Iskoort in various permutations, none of whom seemed to be having an especially good time.

My brain was buzzing. Going a mile a minute, but going nowhere. Like a car with the pedal all the way down but up on blocks, wheels spinning but staying still.

What was I missing? Something. Something. Some way to defeat the Howlers. Had to be some way. The Ellimist didn't send us into this battle to lose.

Did he?

I tried calling to him with my mind. I wondered if he was listening. Probably. But he and Crayak had their rules. The rules of engagement, as the military guys say.

What were the rules? Might as well have that ant look up at the chess grandmaster and demand an explanation for why he'd moved a particular pawn.

Why the Iskoort? Why did they have to be saved? Why had we known we were going after the Howlers, but the Howlers hadn't seemed to know they were going after us till we met on the stairs?

Why didn't the Howlers go after the Iskoort? That was easy: the rules of engagement. If they beat us, they could annihilate the Iskoort. Not until.

The one person we figured could fight and win against the Howlers was Erek. Only Erek had the power. And only Erek was unable to fight. He could put himself between us and the Howlers. He could give us information, but not directly help us.

The Howlers had never lost a battle. That's what the Howler memories and Erek had said. *Never.*

What did it all mean? I pressed my hands hard against my head, like I wanted to squeeze the answer out of my brain.

<We are there,> Guide announced.

I looked up, startled to realize I'd been walking along the whole time. I felt a surge of guilt. I'd been so preoccupied, I hadn't been on guard.

We were standing outside a building shaped like a pyramid, maybe ten stories high in Earth terms. It was white, the gleaming, artificial white of plastic, and featured a wide, arched door outlined in rows of neon, like a rainbow. Something that must have been music was blaring.

"Yeah, this'll be a good place to hide," Marco said sardonically. "No one would ever notice this."

"Where are we, Guide?"

<We have reached the temple of the Servant Guild. They will take you in. I have paid for it. They will care for you until I return.>

"What do you mean, return?" Rachel snapped. "Where are you going?"

<I must feed. You see, we Iskoort are not precisely what we seem at first. The body you see is of our symbiote. We are a symbiotic species — a large outer body, the *Isk*, and the inner self, the much smaller portion, called the *Yoort*.>

<A symbiote?> Ax demanded, speaking for the first time. <Do you mean that you are parasites?>

<Long ago, yes,> Guide acknowledged. <But what began as a parasitic relationship has become a truly symbiotic one. We function as a single creature. The two parts, halves, only separate every three days, when the Yoort must feed by swimming in the Yoort pool and absorbing —>

Ax's tail was at the Iskoort's throat before he could form the next word.

<Yeerks. They're all Yeerks!>

CHAPTER 17

The Servant Guild was just what it sounded like. Slavishly obedient, fawning, groveling Iskoort, fanatically obsessed with obeying your every order, catering to your every whim.

It took a long time for us to convey that all we wanted was a room. A room with none of them in it. They weren't happy about it, but in the end they obeyed.

The room was as gaudy as the exterior of the Servant Guild Temple. The walls were so glaringly white they seemed to make your eyeballs vibrate. What wasn't white was neon, or something like neon, in bold primary colors swirled here and there, up walls and across ceilings and inset in the floor. But the colored light did not seem to touch the whiteness.

"Must be the Iskoort idea of interior decorating," Rachel said. "Like a hospital bathroom decorated by kids with those light wand things."

Guide stood in the middle of the room. Ax had drawn his tail blade back, but Guide was not under any illusions: That tail would snap in a split second if we heard the wrong answers.

"You'd better talk, and talk fast," I told Guide.

He was whining continuously from his diaphragm. <What do you want from me?>

Marco said, "We're a bazillion miles from home, clear across the galaxy, and all of a sudden we find out you Iskoort are Yeerks. Excuse us for being suspicious."

<We are not Yeerks. We are Iskoort.>

<Yoort, Yeerk, that's pretty close,> Tobias said, flaring his wings angrily. <And you both live off Kandrona rays.>

<Yes, we feed on Kandrona rays. But we are Iskoort, not these Yeerks you despise.>

Rachel glared at the cringing Iskoort. "I knew there was something I didn't like about these creeps. If they're not trying to buy something from you, they're trying to kick your butt or kiss your feet. Yeerks!" She turned to me, expression hard.

"That's it. We tell the Ellimist to find someone else to play his games with. We're not helping save a bunch of Yeerks. The Howlers can have them."

I was inclined to agree. It was the easy way out, anyway. We weren't going to die to help Yeerks.

Cassie moved between Guide and Ax. "Guide, tell me something. What do you know about the history of your people? Going way back to the beginning?"

Guide looked bewildered, but Cassie was staying between him and the Andalite's tail, so he knew she was his best hope.

<We . . . we Iskoort . . . I mean, back many, many generations, the Yoort were parasites, as you said. They infested other species. But that was long ago. Since we formed our symbiotes, the combination of Isk and Yoort, we have been as we are now.>

Rachel snorted. "They conquered these Isk things and now it's like okay, we're best buddies. Big deal."

Marco nodded agreement. "Some stranger shows up on Earth a thousand years after the Yeerks conquer Earth, the Yeerks will be saying, 'Hey, us and the humans are symbiotes.'"

I looked at Cassie. Rachel and Marco were right. Cassie nodded, accepting the fact.

But Guide said, <No, no. I have not made myself clear. The Isk were not conquered by the Yoort. They were created.>

"Say what?"

<Parasitism is a limiting choice. The Yoort moved violently to conquer other species and infest them, but this was not profitable, not in the long haul. So the Yoort used biological engineering techniques to design and create a species specifically to be a symbiote.>

<Who cares how you did it?> Tobias argued. <So you build the Isk and then enslave them.>

<No, no,> Guide pleaded, whining away through his diaphragm. <The Isk were true symbiotes. The Isk cannot live without the Yoort. And to ensure that this symbiosis would be real, the Yoort, too, were modified. Now Yoort cannot live without Isk and Isk cannot live without Yoort. They are one creature with two parts.>

Dead silence. No one said a thing. The reality of it was sinking slowly into our suspicious brains.

"Oh, my God," Cassie said at last. "Of course. It's the way. The *only* way. Parasite becomes symbiote. No more infestation. They create the next step in their own evolution and become true symbiotes."

"No more war," Erek said quietly. "No more

93

need to conquer new species, to infest and en-slave."

"The Yeerks don't know about this," Cassie said. "Even the Yeerks who want peace cannot imagine a way out, a way to end the cycle of con-quest."

<These Yoort could be related to the Yeerks,> Ax said. <They may be the same species, some-how separated long ago, perhaps carried from the Yeerk home world by some forgotten race.>

<If the Yeerks knew . . . if the Iskoort ever made contact with the Yeerks . . .> Tobias said.

This was why Crayak had to destroy the Iskoort. And why the Ellimist couldn't allow it. Someday, maybe far in the future, Iskoort would meet Yeerk. And the Yeerks would see that there was another way.

I smiled. The first time in a long time. The ant had just figured out part of the chess game.

CHAPTER 18

A smell like oil and mothballs and . . .

"It's poison!" Rachel said. "Like bug poison."

<Howlers!> Tobias yelled.

What to do? The Howlers were pumping poison into the building. They had learned fast. Too fast. Insect morphs were no longer available.

"Guide! Windows?"

<Yes, there are windows concealed. I can open them by —>

"Not yet. We go airborne," I told everyone. "Stay calm. Morph to bird. Guide, when I say, open the windows. Not before. The Howlers won't come in till they're sure they've spread enough poison."

I tried to sound confident. I hoped I was right.

95

The stench of poison was growing stronger by the second, but I was already on my way to morphing a peregrine falcon.

Why bug poison? Why not nerve gas? Why not some odorless, invisible gas that would kill us before we knew what hit us?

Too easy? Not enough fear factor for the Howlers? Or was no deadly gas one of the rules of engagement?

We were melting, all but Erek and Guide. Morphing. Flesh oozing and shifting like mud sliding down a hill. Flesh turned gray. Arms and legs broke out in feather patterns. Faces crumpled, then extruded hard beaks. Toes became talons.

<Guide, how high up are we?>

<Perhaps five times your own height.>

<Okay. Erek, we don't know if any Howler is sitting outside that window. Maybe yes, maybe no. Can you jump through it, push whoever's there out of the way?>

Erek looked sick. "No, Jake. I can hear the Howlers. I know they're out there. If I go through that window I might harm —"

<Wouldn't want that,> Marco sneered. <We wouldn't want —>

<Shut up, Marco,> I rapped. My mind was racing. Some answer. There had to be. We needed a distraction, otherwise, the instant we appeared,

the Howlers would . . . <Erek! Can you project a hologram through another window? A hologram of us?>

"Absolutely. There would be no harm to the Howlers, and it might save you. That would be well within my parameters."

<Guide, open a window on the far side of the room, count to three, and open this one over here. Guide, Erek? We hook up two levels down, near the stairs. Everyone ready?>

<Two levels down?> Guide said, looking startled.

Just then a pair of Servant Iskoort came bustling into the room. <Is there a problem? Are those guests clinging to the outside of the building disturbing your rest?>

<Make it fast,> Tobias said, ignoring the intrusion. <Birds don't tolerate poison much better than bugs do.>

<Point taken. On three. One, two, NOW!>

The far window slid open. Instantly a flight of six birds flew toward it. Dracon beams burned and flechette guns rattled.

<Yes, let us open the windows,> one of the Servant Iskoort offered.

<Perhaps a delightful meal?>

The near window opened and I spread my wings and flapped with all my panicky strength.

The hologram broke down after extending a

97

couple of dozen feet from the window. But by then all seven Howlers were firing like idiots on the wrong side of the building.

We blew out of the window, flapping like mad, desperate for every foot of distance. But we were not far when the first Dracon beam singed Rachel's eagle wing.

<Down, down, down!> I yelled.

We dove. Down into the maze of trees and bushes and flowers. We were a weird squadron. A bald eagle, a pair of ospreys, a northern harrier, a red-tailed hawk, and a peregrine falcon.

We blazed along the lane, inches above the heads of walking Iskoort. They'd feel our wind and look up as we passed.

B-r-r-r-r-r-r-t-t!

A line of flechettes tore a tree apart inches ahead of me.

I turned left and saw the Howler. He was racing after us, knocking Iskoort down like they were so many bowling pins.

We turned a sharp left, banking around a line of fuzzy orange trees. A Howler burst from the vegetation ahead of us! He had torn through the planters to cut us off.

<Pull up!> Tobias yelled.

TSEEEEW! TSEEEEEW!

Cassie's right wing was gone, a burning rag falling to the ground! Cassie tumbled, out of control, falling like a stone. She hit the ground amidst a gaggle of Warmaker Iskoort.

I dived after her.

A Howler jumped from an overhanging tree. He aimed his beam weapon even as he plummeted toward Cassie's still, crumpled form.

TSEEEEW! TSEEEEW!

He fired, missed! Landed. I was on him, talons forward. I raked bloody lines across his head. He twisted his turntable body and aimed at me.

I carried through, lost momentum, and slammed into one of the Warmaker Iskoort. The Iskoort stared blankly at me. I was in his arms. Helpless.

The Howler grinned and took careful aim. Right at me. No chance to escape. Point-blank range. Inches away. I could see every detail of the weapon that would end my life.

Then . . . the Dracon beam wavered. It rose. I saw the Howler's face, furious, enraged. But he did not fire.

I flapped my wings. The Warmaker Iskoort reacted by shoving me away angrily, and then he and his fellows attacked the Howler.

It should have been over in an instant. The Warmaker Iskoort were not exactly formidable. The Howler should have laid them out in five seconds. Instead, the Howler shielded himself from attack, pushing back the thrusting, butting heads, and ran.

Rules of engagement!

<They can't kill the Iskoort!> I yelled to the others. <Use the Iskoort for cover!> Then, <Cassie! Cassie, if you can hear me, demorph! Demorph!>

But I could already see her flesh growing from the missing, burned scar where her wing had been. <Yeah, yeah, I know,> she said, sounding stunned.

<Ax! Behind you!>

<Here comes another one!>

The others were running for their lives. I had to get to them. <Cassie. Are you okay?>

<I'll . . . you know . . . uh . . . demorph,> she said, dazed, lost.

<Cassie, demorph! And stay close to the Iskoort!>

<Yeah. Yeah.>

<I can't leave you like this!>

<No. Yes. Go. You have to —>

A Howler was bounding toward me, his dead blue eyes focused on me. If I stayed, I'd lead him to Cassie. If I left . . . I couldn't leave her! She was too dazed, losing too much blood, sinking too fast to finish demorphing.

No choice, Jake, I told myself harshly. *You can't help. You can only hurt.*

I flapped away, feeling like my heart was being ripped from my body. I gained enough altitude to get above the trees, where I saw a bizarre battle under way.

Have to help the others, I told myself. *That's your duty. Help them. You can't help Cassie anymore.*

The Howlers were leaping from tree to tree, like monkeys on steroids. They were simply leaping across the walkways, vine to bush to branch, like people crossing a stream by jumping from rock to rock.

I saw three birds in the air. One missing besides Cassie. The edge of the platform, the void, was only a mile away.

<Okay,> I said. <I've had enough of this. They want to chase someone? Let's see just how fast they are.>

CHAPTER 19

The peregrine falcon is the fastest animal on Earth. Faster than the cheetah or gazelle. Faster than the fastest dolphin or shark. Faster than any bird. In a dive it can break two hundred miles an hour.

I flapped, up, up, up, burning energy like I didn't care, and I didn't. I wouldn't be needing energy for later. There wasn't going to be a later. Cassie down. Rachel down. I felt sick inside.

But I was going to take a Howler with me.

I flew hard and fast and caught a little help from a headwind that I rode like a skateboarder going up the side of a pipe.

Then I took careful aim, judged the distance, and dived.

I didn't reach two hundred miles an hour, but I was breaking a hundred by the time I slashed the top of a Howler who was ripping after Tobias.

The Howler grabbed his head, howling a more emotional and less dangerous howl than the one he was named for. He fired wildly at me, but I was out of there.

I kept most of my momentum and banked right, flapping hard, then raked a Howler who had just dropped Marco with a burst of flechettes.

<Marco!> I cried. <Demorph! Demorph!>

I couldn't tell if he was still alive. But I could see his assailant. He got a face full of razor-sharp talon. I aimed for his eyes.

The Howlers had never been beaten. I wondered how they liked what I was doing to them.

I got my answer immediately. Three of them converged, racing toward me, flinging themselves forward in mad, heedless pursuit of the little creature who had dared to hurt them.

Not too fast, Jake, I told myself. I flew, but not at full speed. Rather, I used my speed to dodge and weave and frustrate the Howlers who fired everything they had at me.

Close enough, I thought. Now, down! I dropped below tree-level, down to the walkway. But here the walkway was almost devoid of Iskoort.

I stuck to the path, fighting exhaustion, flapping, turning, flapping, turning. And the Howlers were after me. They ripped through the hedges, blew trees apart with flechettes, burned flowers and bushes out of their path.

I was going up and down a circuitous path. They were cutting straight through. In seconds they would cut me off. I couldn't outrun them when I had to travel ten feet for every one foot of theirs.

But I had to stay down. Had to stay on the path. Had to hope I was right about direction and distance. Had to hope the Howlers' arrogance, the cockiness of the never-defeated, would help me.

Turn, turn, turn!

Around I came. A Howler burst through the hedge just in front of me! Trapped!

Was I right? Was I there?

I went straight at the Howler. He aimed. I jerked suddenly upward and dropped slowly, like a wounded bird, like a slow, loopy volleyball, over the hedge to the far side.

The Howler ripped through the hedge, smelling victory.

He ripped through and clawed at the air.

The Iskoort were crazy not to put guardrails around the edges of their platforms.

But it was a kind of crazy I could get to like.

The Howler fell. Fell, clawing the air, scream-ing in rage and frustration. Miles above the ground. He had a long way to fall.

And then it hit me. Now was the time.

I was in the right place and in the right morph.

Down he fell, quickly achieving maximum falling velocity. Which in the gravity of the Iskoort world, as it turned out, was less than two hundred miles an hour.

CHAPTER 20

Down, down, down.

The Howler was facedown, yelling and grabbing air. Helpless.

I flew straight down, flapping hard, helping gravity work. The Howler was right below me, oblivious.

He had other things on his mind.

I folded my wings back, brought my talons forward, and latched on to his leg. If he felt my sharp talons, he didn't show it.

I looked past him at the ground so far below. How long would it take us to fall? Long enough? No way to know. Had to try.

I began to demorph. We were falling at the same speed now, the Howler and I. I tried to hold on to him as my talons became fingers, as my body grew and grew almost as large as his. I tried to hold on to that half-cooled lava skin. But my talons slipped as the claws became fingernails. I lost my grip.

I grabbed again with a stubby hand and an arm eight inches long. Missed. We fell. My eyes lost their falcon focus. I could no longer see every detail of the ground far below me. It was a blur. It made it seem further away. A small comfort.

Human, I fell, my face just inches from the Howler's left leg. He had stopped clawing the air. He was no longer moving. He had a long time to contemplate his fate. I didn't feel sorry for him. Maybe I should have. Maybe Cassie would have.

But this Howler, or one just like him, had burned her wing off. Had shot Marco. At least one of the others. Maybe all of them by now.

I wanted him to have a nice, long time to think about that as he fell.

I grabbed, this time with human fingers.

He swiveled suddenly, turned his body all the way around, and stared down at me, his blank blue eyes wide with shock.

He reached for his Dracon beam. I snatched it first and threw it away. It fell, twirling beside us, five feet away and a million miles out of reach.

I knew what was coming next. But the Howler didn't. He started his howl, the first notes ear-splitting, brain-numbing.

KEEEE —

But he was too late. I had begun to acquire him. And he felt the torpor, the lethargy that creatures usually feel when acquired. He stared, eyes full of hate, unable to raise his deadly howl.

While I kept my grip on him, while I drained his DNA into me, I used my free hand to strip away his weapons. One by one. They made a small arsenal falling around us.

I pushed away. The air caught me and spun me end over end. I windmilled my arms, trying to stabilize, but it was a foolish instinct. I calmed down and began to morph.

The ground was close now. Close, so close. It was as if at the end we were moving faster and faster, as if the last half of the fall took only a tenth as long as the first half.

Fear distorts reality. Reality was plenty dis-torted.

I tumbled wildly, seeing the ground sweep by beneath me one minute, then the Howler above me. My shove had set him tumbling, too. It was all that saved me, because he began to howl.

KEEEEEEEEEEE-row!

But the blasts of sound only hit me glancing blows as we spun like a pair of suicidal sky divers.

I felt the itchiness of feathers growing from my skin.

The ground, so close!

Hard beak pushed out from my lips.

The ground! Rushing up now. Grim, scruffy trees and drifting, ground-hugging fog.

My arms were shriveling, the bones thinning, hollowing.

Too late!

KEEEEEEEEEEE-row!

A thousand feet!

Five hundred!

One hundred feet!

Treetops rising around me!

I opened my wings. I felt them fill and strain, the muscles almost tearing with the effort.

The Howler fell away from me.

<Tell the Big Red Eye that Jake says "hi,"> I said.

My wings filled and I flew at impossible speed across the treetops.

CHAPTER 21

I could see why the Iskoort had built their Dr. Seuss towers. The surface of the planet was a reeking, swampy mess of a place. I gained altitude to get above the sulfur smell, but then had to rest.

My falcon body was revived by remorphing, but it was a several-mile ascent to get back to where I'd left the others. And how was I ever going to find that level? The structure of the Iskoort city was unimaginably complex.

Flying outside of it, I could see just what an awesome structure it was. Nothing ever built on Earth even came close. The pyramids would not have made the footing for the smallest pillar at the base of this thing. The World Trade Center and the Sears Tower were Tinkertoys.

The Iskoort may have been the most obnoxious species in the galaxy, but they could definitely build.

What would I find when I did manage to retrace my fall? Had Cassie demorphed? Had she survived? Was Marco still alive? Ax, Tobias, Rachel?

They'd been hopelessly outgunned. Part of me expected to find that the score would be one Howler, and all five of my friends. I pictured finding their crumpled bodies. The images drained the strength from my muscles.

I had to get back. But I couldn't stand thinking about what I'd find. I couldn't live without them. Couldn't.

I felt a surge of anger at Erek. Marco was right: What right did Erek have to cling to his nonviolence in a universe where the Howlers annihilated entire species on orders from an evil force? How do you stand on the sidelines when evil is running amok?

Erek was the only one of us who could fight a Howler and win. He had the power. He alone had the power. We'd freed him for one hour from his peaceful programming. The result had been terrifying. He had annihilated a Yeerk force that would have destroyed us all.

111

Yes, the Pemalites had created him and all his kind to be peaceful. To be physically incapable of violence. And it was irrational of me to be angry. But with Cassie and Rachel and maybe everyone dead and me alone, I didn't care.

The Pemalites were fools. They'd been wiped out by the Howlers while their incredibly powerful androids had stood by and done nothing.

The Pemalites had not reprogrammed the Chee. Idiots! The Chee could have saved them. The Chee could have been turned loose to destroy the Howlers the way the Howlers destroyed everyone else. And then . . .

And then, when the Chee had destroyed the Howlers, what would they do next? What do you do with a species devoted to war? What do you do, once you've created an awesome weapon and turned it loose?

The Pemalites would have had to be sure they could rein in the Chee. They would have had to be sure they could control them. Turn them off.

Just as Crayak would need a way to control the Howlers.

The Howlers weren't androids, so how did Crayak ensure that they would never get out of control? And since their job was to murder and murder and murder without pity, what would Crayak even think "out of control" would mean?

Out of control for a Howler would be not killing.

An out-of-control Howler would be a Howler who felt remorse. Pity. Kindness. That would be intolerable to Crayak.

I laughed bitterly. Nice speculation. But my friends were probably all dead. And I was alone. And all I could hope for now was to live long enough to get home again.

<Jake! Is that you, or some other peregrine falcon?>

<Tobias!>

<Yeah. I've been looking for you.>

<You're alive!>

<Same back at you, fearless leader,> he said with a laugh. <We figured you were done for. Ax saw you go over the side with that Howler.>

<Is everyone . . . is anyone . . .>

Tobias sounded less ebullient. <We're all still there, but it wasn't pretty. Cassie, Rachel, and Marco all got nailed pretty bad. But they all managed to demorph. Erek caught up with us and created a hologram of Iskoort. Cassie said you told her the Howlers couldn't attack Iskoort. Guess that's why they didn't howl.>

<But everyone's okay?> I pressed, unable to fully believe it.

Tobias laughed. <Yeah, big Jake, everyone's alive. Anyway, we got everyone inside the

113

hologram and the Howlers seemed stumped. But I guess they figured out we weren't really Iskoort, so it was okay to attack. By then we were assorted bugs crawling around the trees. Guide found us another place. Wait till you see. How about your Howler?>

<It's not teams of seven anymore. It's seven to six now,> I said.

Fortunately, Tobias had kept track of where he was. He easily led the way back to a level three stories down from where we'd been.

This level was different than any we'd seen thus far. It seemed to be an industrial district. The separation from the floor above was several hundred feet. The predominating colors were gray and brown. And the factories, if that's what they were, looked as drab and windowless and shabby as any factories on Earth.

Here, as we flew above them, we met a new variation on the Iskoort. These had longer, stronger arms, more massive shoulders, and their eyes were hooded with thick, retractable lids.

There were very few out and about. Those I saw, though, seemed boisterously happy and oblivious to the grimness around them. But their whining diaphragms were so loud that a small group of them whining together could make you long for earplugs.

We circled around a few times, looking for

Howlers. But they were not in sight. We landed. I demorphed and went inside.

I thought I was past the emotion. I thought I was over that feeling of hollowness I'd felt, imagining them all gone. But then there they were.

Rachel scowling. Marco looking down at the floor, withdrawn. Ax off by himself, still no doubt blaming himself. Erek with his hologram turned off, an unemotional android face.

And Cassie.

<Prince Jake!> Ax cried, the first to see me.

Cassie was on her feet and running toward me, and I was running to her, and I wasn't past any emotion, I was exploding with emotion.

Cassie jumped into my arms and I wrapped her up tight and before I knew it I was kissing her on her lips and she was kissing me back.

"It's about time," Rachel grumbled.

CHAPTER 22

At least Cassie and I provided Marco with material. It took him precisely three seconds after I parted from Cassie, embarrassed and amazed.

He held out his arms to me and said, "What, no kiss for me?"

I would not have believed I could feel like a dork in the middle of all the other feelings I was dealing with, and in the middle of an abject disaster of a battle, but I guess embarrassment and awkwardness are always with us.

"No?" Marco said, looking puzzled. "I guess I'll have to turn to Rachel." He went for her, arms out, lips puckered.

"Gee, Marco, what do you think the odds are

I'll kiss you? Slim, none, or I'll-break-both-your-arms?"

I looked around at our latest home. It was a large open space, maybe three stories high, about the size of a basketball court. Crammed into that gloomy cube were an amazing array of machines. Some like giant jackhammers, some like steel octopi, others weirdly like merry-go-rounds with elaborate, sharp-edged tools instead of brightly colored horses.

Nothing was working. There was dust everywhere.

"Abandoned factory?" I asked Guide.

<Not abandoned. The Worker Guild refuses to come back to work here until the Superstition and Magic Guild certifies that the place is free of the spirits of fictional characters.>

I sighed. I hesitated. I shot a look at Marco.

"Oh, you'll want to hear this," he said.

"What are the spirits of fictional characters?"

Guide whined in what I took to be a humorous way. <The simple folk believe that fictional characters are at least partly real and thus have spirits who wander the city, infesting buildings and engaging in various destructive behaviors.>

"Fictional characters," I said. "Okay."

<So naturally, the Superstition and Magic Guild must be called upon to control this problem.

But the Worker Guild cannot agree on a fair price, so . . .>

"Makes perfect sense," I said.

"In a loony bin," Rachel said.

We all fell silent for a while. The rush of being reunited was wearing off. We were remembering reality.

<Jake says it's seven to six now,> Tobias said.

"Swell," Marco muttered. "Make it seven to two and I'd still bet on them."

There was muttered agreement.

"I have a new morph," I said.

<Yeah?> Tobias asked.

"Yeah. On the way . . . on the way down, I acquired the Howler. It's not enough, but it may give us an edge. If we have an overall plan."

"Do you have a plan?" Erek asked.

I considered. Did I? I had bits and pieces. Guesses. Speculation. Intuitions.

I shrugged. "Yeah. I guess I do."

Marco grinned. "Kiss him again, Cassie. It seems to help."

They all waited expectantly. I bowed my head and tried to bring together all that I had learned about the Howlers. I felt like I had a bunch of jigsaw pieces and no picture to work from.

"Okay, jump in if you have anything to add. I could be totally wrong. One: The Howlers must have some kind of collective memory. The memories Erek absorbed were of events going back thousands of years and covering dozens of invasions. No biological creature lives that long. And we know the Howlers are biological because I acquired one. So somehow, the Howlers are designed to share a single memory. What these seven Howlers . . . six . . . learn here will be conveyed to all the rest of the species. That way all battle experience is available to all warriors."

Rachel nodded. "No wonder they never lose."

"Yeah, but that brings up something else. See, no one wins all the time. Not for thousands of years. It's not possible. Muhammad Ali lost. Michael Jordan lost. No one wins every time."

"But the Howler memories I absorbed show no memory of defeat," Erek pointed out.

"Yeah. Exactly," I said. "Exactly. Guide?"

<Yes?>

"When you view memories — I mean in the normal way, not like Erek did for us, turning it into a hologram — how is it done?"

Guide emitted a low diaphragm whine and said, <There is a small device that attaches to the head. It ties in directly to brain waves and plays the memories as if you yourself were recalling them.>

"And these memory headsets work on all species?"

<We are visited by many species,> Guide

said. <The headsets have always worked. Although not all species choose to indulge.>

"I'm guessing the Howlers don't indulge," Cassie said.

Guide spread his hands and increased the grating noise from his diaphragm. <We have only ever seen this one group of Howlers. They sold their memories to pay for what they needed here, but they did not choose to buy any other memories.>

I nodded. "Good. Good. Okay. Now we need a volunteer for an extremely dangerous mission. We're going to need a rabbit to draw the hounds to us." I shot a look at Rachel and slowly shook my head no. Her mouth was already open to volunteer. She closed it and looked puzzled.

<I will take on this mission,> Ax said from across the room.

Rachel made a little half-smile and nodded imperceptibly.

"Swell," Marco said impatiently. "So Ax is going to get himself killed and we all agree the Howlers don't like to buy memories to watch on their VCRs. How does any of this let us take out these six Howlers?"

"We don't take out the six Howlers," I said. "Crayak does."

CHAPTER 23

The place we were in was all wrong for the trap. We needed Iskoort around us. We had to make the rules of engagement work for us. I explained it to Guide. He wanted to get paid more. We were running up a big bill, and we might well get killed before we could sell him our valuable memories.

"Don't worry," I said. "That's the next thing we do: make a complete copy of our memories."

<I still feel I should be able to harvest an arm, at the least. Perhaps some minor internal organ.>

"Not more hair?"

<I have the hair,> he said. <The point is to

possess what is absolutely unique. No one has a human body part or organ.>

"Yeah, and it's going to stay that way," I said. "You can have Marco's hair."

"Say what?"

<A stalk eye from the Andalite?>

"No. No body parts. We had a deal."

<What if you should be killed?> Guide asked, lowering his whine to an annoying whimper.

"You want our bodies?" I demanded, shocked, despite the fact that I had bigger problems to worry about. "If you were doing organ transplants to save lives, yeah, but just so you can stick us in big pickle jars and charge admission to see the human freaks? I don't think so."

"I have something to sell," Erek said. "I will create a schematic of my holographic technology. You can build your own emitters."

This was apparently such a bonanza that Guide stopped whining for several seconds. He barely managed to say, <Deal!>

Marco rolled his eyes. "You know, Guide is going to own this planet by the time he's done."

Guide led us to a different level. This time we went up. And this time we took an elevator.

"Elevators! You have elevators?" Marco raged. "We're traipsing up and down stairs and you have elevators?"

<The elevators are much less scenic,> Guide

122

said. <What value are memories of the inside of an elevator?>

We emerged several floors above the one where we'd first appeared. It was just what I needed: narrow walkways between tall residential buildings with shops on the ground level. Iskoort crammed everywhere. Iskoort mostly of a new type: Shopper Iskoort.

"My people!" Rachel cried in delight. "At last I have a true homeland!"

"They shop?" I asked Guide. "That's it? They shop?"

<Someone must buy what is created in the great factories and small craftworks,> Guide said.

"Exactly," Rachel agreed.

<The economy cannot function without people to buy things.>

"Guide, you are finally making sense," Rachel said with great satisfaction.

We went to an empty store at the end of a long, narrow street. The previous business had moved out, leaving nothing but empty shelves behind.

"Okay. This will do," I said. "Now. How do we get the word to the Howlers that we're here?"

<I have only to mention it to a member of the News, Gossip, and Speculation Guild,> Guide said.

123

<This is quite a little lunatic asylum the El­imist wants us to save,> Tobias said. <Lego Land meets Dr. Seuss with a population made up of whining nutbags — no offense, Guide — who think shopping and gossiping are careers.>

"Hey, don't diss my brothers and sisters of the Shopper Guild," Rachel said with mock ferocity.

"Okay, let's get this in gear," I said. "Guide? We have the memory players?"

<Yes, of course.>

"Ax? You ready?"

<Yes, Prince Jake,> he said.

"Don't call me Prince. And come here for a minute." I went into an empty corner with him. "Ax, maybe I'm wrong, but you still seem to be chafing over that first battle."

<I ran away,> he said simply.

"You came back."

<I ran away,> he repeated harshly.

"You were the only one not in morph. You and Tobias. And he was in the air, not close to that howling noise. Does it occur to you that maybe the Howler's howl is specially designed to affect the brains of sentient creatures? I mean, the physical brain, the gray matter — or whatever color yours is?"

He shrugged impatiently, a gesture he'd picked up from humans.

"Listen, Ax, the Howlers are a biological weapon designed to kill sentient species. When they were designed, when Crayak was coming up with that howl, he'd have fine-tuned it to have an especially terrifying effect on complex, sentient brains. I had a tiger brain and it nearly destroyed me. You had your own, very smart, very aware, very complex brain. Exactly what the howl was designed to attack."

Ax didn't accept what I was saying. But he didn't dismiss it totally, either. He seemed to fidget, like he wished the conversation was over.

I sighed. I'd said all I could say. Ax needed to do something to wipe away what he saw as a terrible stain.

"Okay, Ax. It's time to get set. But you better remember one thing: Your job is to get out of this alive. If I'm really your prince, I'll give you an order: You do not have permission to get yourself killed. No matter how heroic you think it would be."

CHAPTER 24

It took less than an hour.

Tobias, floating high above the narrow streets, saw them burst at a run from the stairs. They looked around, knowing the floor we were on, but not the building.

We didn't want them having time to plan. We wanted to use their blood-lust and rage.

Down the street, seemingly oblivious, walked Ax. Tobias reported the scene by thought-speak.

<He's almost there. The Howlers are sticking together. Not as cocky as they were, though. They should spot him any second now. Any second now.>

Then, <What are they, blind? Ax is getting awfully close. The crowd is blocking their view of

him. Too many Iskoort in the way. Oh, man! He's too . . . They see him! Ax-man, run! Run!>

I looked at Cassie and the others. "It's time. I have to do this."

I blocked images of Ax from my mind. Images of him racing, dodging, weaving through the Iskoort crowds. Images of the Howlers bounding after him.

Instead, I focused on a different image: the Howler I had acquired. I formed the image in my mind and I felt the changes begin.

"Rachel," I said, while I was still human, "you know what to do. If I get out of control, can't control the morph. If I start that howl . . . you'll have to do it."

Rachel had morphed to grizzly bear. She stood directly behind me. Her two massive front paws, with claws that could flay the bark off a tree, lay on my shoulders.

If I lost control of the morph, Rachel would . . . would do what she had to do. Quickly. Before I could hurt anyone.

As backup, Marco was in gorilla morph. His fist, as big as my head, and powered by enough muscle to knock a hole in a wall, was cocked a foot from my face.

<They're on him!> Tobias yelled. <All six of them. Like hounds after a rabbit. Man! That boy can run! Ax-man! Opening to your right!>

The Howlers could not shoot, not in a crowd of Iskoort. Rules of engagement. Nor could they use their howls, not without possibly killing Iskoort.

But if they got close enough to Ax, then would come the flechette guns, the Dracon beams, and the knives.

I steadied my thoughts. *Control. Control.*

The morph continued. My skin began to erupt in pustules, blisters that formed all over my body, then burst and oozed out black glue.

I looked down and saw my stomach pinching, like I was being cut in two. Like I was morphing an ant or some other segmented insect. Just as the pinching looked as if it would go all the way and the top of my body would topple like a chopped tree, long, flexible threads — elastic blood veins — shot out, connecting the two halves of me, upper and lower.

For a horrible moment I could actually see the white bone of my human spine. The interlocking vertebrae melted and reformed as thick, steel-gray cylinders, each able to turn on its base.

Then my center filled in, hiding the spine and the elastic veins and tendons.

I breathed a sigh of relief. No one needs to see that happening to their body.

I saw my hands change color, the fingers cov-ered by the black-on-red pustules, the cooling lava flesh thick and hard. I still had four fingers and a thumb. But now, from my wrist, the claws grew. Retractable, like a cat's claws.

My legs creaked and groaned as bone thickened and twisted. My ears melted into my head. My eyes widened, growing larger and flatter.

My senses began to change. The differences were not as severe as many morphs I've been through. But more complete than I'd expected. I wasn't seeing just shape and color anymore. I was seeing infrared heat. I was seeing trails, like the ones your mouse cursor leaves on the computer screen. It allowed me to follow movement and direction more closely.

And then, with a shock, I realized I could see through the outer layers of skin. I could see faint outlines of Marco's gorilla heart.

Of course. All the better to target vital organs.

The robin's egg blue-in-blue eyes were far beyond human eyes. Beyond even hawk's eyes. These were target-acquiring eyes.

Suddenly, I felt it bubble up from beneath my own consciousness. I had expected rage. I had expected out-of-control violent urges. I felt neither. Instead, I felt . . . indifference.

There was no Howler instinct to slaughter. It wasn't anger. That wasn't how they were built.

Crayak had been more subtle than that. I had

expected the Howler morph to be like morphing some superpredator. But the morph this reminded me of most was the dolphin.

Howlers were playful.

Howlers were having fun.

<You can let me go,> I told Rachel and Marco.

<Are you sure?>

<Yeah. This thing isn't out of control. It's like . . .

And then I felt something I had never felt before. Some strange part of the Howler brain, like an extra sense. My brain had tapped into a pool of awareness, of knowledge.

Rapid, dizzying flashes of memory. Horrifying images of slaughter, violence. Not just the Graffen's Children. But species after species. Planet after planet. I was getting the full, horrific imagery that Erek had absorbed in a different way.

But this was worse. This wasn't someone else's memory. This was my own. It was part of me.

And through it all, the massacre of Graffen's Children, the slaughter of the Mashtimee, the Pon, the Nostnavay, and yes, the Pemalites, the Howlers felt no anger, no rage.

But why should they?

<It's a game,> I said.

<What is?> Cassie asked. She had morphed to wolf.

<The Howlers. The killing. It's a game to them. They're having fun. They're enjoying it. Like when dolphin leap into the air just for the fun of it and play follow the leader, it's a game.>

<They're destroying entire races for fun?>

<Yes. They don't know what they're doing. Cassie . . . they aren't adults. The Howlers are all children.>

131

CHAPTER 25

<Here they come!> Tobias yelled. <Thirty seconds. If —>

<Children, my butt,> Rachel said. <They're murderers!>

<They're what Crayak made them,> I said. <They have a life span of three years. They have no mature phase. They don't reproduce; they're grown in a factory. There are no adult Howlers.>

I looked hard at Erek. <Did you know?>

"Before? No."

<When you absorbed Howler memories, did you realize they are children?> I demanded.

"They slaughtered my creators," Erek said stonily.

<Crowd is thinning out, Ax-man!> Tobias yelled. <They're gonna have a shot!>

<So what, we let them walk away, just because they're not adults?> Marco demanded.

<It's not going to be up to us,> I said grimly. <If the plan works, Crayak will —>

<It's not just Crayak,> Cassie said. <We're the ones forcing the —>

The sound of flechette guns, in the street outside our door, only a dozen feet from us.>

<Aaahhhh!> Ax cried in pain.

<He's hit!> Tobias yelled.

"Juveniles or adults, they massacred my creators, they made refugees of the Chee, they murdered my world," Erek said through gritted teeth.

<No choice, man,> Marco said.

<They don't know,> I said. Was I pleading? What did I think we could do? It was too late. Them or us. Them or the entire Iskoort race.

But they didn't know what they were doing! They didn't know! My head was swimming. The Howlers were what someone else had made them. How do you hate a creature for doing what it has been taught to do?

I had gloated when that Howler fell to its death.

And now no choice! No choice!

<Places,> I ordered. <Get ready.>

133

Marco, Cassie, and Rachel all moved swiftly into place. Erek, too. Guide stayed close.

WHAM!

The door blew back on its hinges. Ax stumbled, bleeding, into the room.

The first Howler was two seconds behind him. He bounded into the room.

Rachel, Marco, and Cassie hit him, simply barreling into him.

Erek snatched up Guide like the Iskoort was made of feathers. He jumped to the door. Guide clung to Erek's neck, terrified, as Erek filled the doorway.

The first Howler kicked with shocking power and sent Rachel stumbling back. A swipe of his arm, with retractable claws down, ripped red lines in Cassie's side. She fell. He aimed his flechette gun. Marco hit him from behind. His aim went wild, ripping a line across the wall and up onto the ceiling.

The pursuing Howlers stopped abruptly at the doorway. All together they might dislodge Erek. But Erek was holding Guide.

The rules of engagement! The Howlers could not kill an Iskoort!

The first Howler spun and nailed Marco with a fist. Not till he pulled back did I realize that fist had held a knife. The handle now protruded from Marco's stomach. He stared at it, disbelieving.

And now the Howler steadied his flechette gun, ready to finish Rachel off.

"No!" I yelled.

The Howler looked at me and blinked.

"Forget them! This way!" I ordered.

The Howler was trying to clear his head. He recognized me. But he knew I was dead. Wasn't I?

"Their leader, over here!" I said, desperately hoping against hope he'd buy it. I took off at a trot.

The Howler followed. I almost collapsed from relief.

I stopped suddenly. The Howler stopped, too, wondering what —

I hit him. Once, twice, three times, each blow aimed with Howler eyes, each blow directed at weak spots that only another Howler would recognize.

He was down. Barely.

The other Howlers were solving the Erek and Guide problem. They were burning several new holes in the walls. Guide couldn't be in front of all of them. In seconds, the Howlers would be inside.

<NOW!> I yelled in thought-speak. But Marco was unable to respond. He was transfixed, looking at the knife in his stomach.

<Marco! The memory emitter! Now! He's getting up!>

It was Ax, bleeding and staggering, who suddenly thrust the small, shiny device into my hand.

I gave him a nod, took a deep breath, and slapped the probe onto the Howler's head.

<Time for an education,> I said.

The Howler glared at me with his dead blue eyes. He leaped up. He drew his Dracon beam weapon. He aimed it . . . nowhere.

He shuddered. He started again to aim the weapon. Then he shuddered again.

His eyes closed.

I stopped breathing.

Into the Howler's head flowed all the memories of my life. From vague, early images of my mother's face above my crib, to riding on my dad's back at some amusement park, to school, to friends, to all that had happened since we'd taken a shortcut through an abandoned construction site.

All that I remembered of my life was flowing into the Howler's brain. And the lives of Cassie and Rachel and Marco and Ax and Tobias. And even Guide. And the long, long memory of the android who called himself Erek.

All that we were emptied into that Howler's head. And from there would flow into the endless pool of collective Howler memory.

<Is it working?> Cassie wondered.

Suddenly, the Howler disappeared. He was simply gone.

The Dracon beams no longer burned against the walls of the room.

Erek stuck his head out through the door. "They're gone," he said.

Marco yanked the knife out of his stomach and began to demorph.

In the time it took him to pull it out, we went from that small Iskoort room to a very different place.

CHAPTER 26

He was huge.

No arms. Arms were irrelevant to him.

He sat on what might have been a throne, or might have been a part of him, I couldn't tell.

Machine? Creature? Both?

Or something that was neither.

He turned his single, huge, bloodred eye and looked down at me.

I was on my knees. Human again. Hard steel beneath me. Darkness all around. But I felt a hand touching mine.

The others were with me, too. With me, cowering beneath the seething evil creature called Crayak.

I met his gaze. I closed my eyes, but I could still see him looking at me. As he had watched me, mocking, in my dreams.

"We meet at last, face-to-face," Crayak said, in a low voice that vibrated up through the floor, through the air, a voice so low that it seemed it would shake my very atoms apart.

I kept my eyes turned away, though it did no good. I wanted to stand, but I couldn't. I was shaking. My teeth were chattering.

"What? Not so brave now, little Jake?" he mocked. "Look at you, all of you, cowering! Are you frightened?"

I nodded. "Yeah, I am," I admitted in a weak voice. "But we won."

And then there was a laugh. A laugh that was as powerful as the awesome dread that flowed from Crayak.

The big red eye snapped up, away from me. I breathed again.

The laughter continued, gathering force, louder and louder and more and more delighted.

I turned and saw the Ellimist. He was in human guise, looking like a wise old man. No more his true face than Erek's face was true.

"Humans," the Ellimist said, as if he were introducing us. "Five humans, an Andalite, a Chee."

"It was a mistake allowing the Chee to escape from the doom of their Pemalite masters," Crayak said.

"The Iskoort will live," the Ellimist said.

The eye showed no expression. "The Iskoort will live."

Then he looked at me. "Sleep well, human," he sneered. "I'll still be there in your dreams. And someday, when the time is right, you will suffer for this."

I climbed to my feet, still holding Cassie's hand. I focused my mind on the Howler. And I began to morph.

No one said anything till I was done. And when I was done, I opened my Howler mind to the collective memory that linked them all.

I searched for the memories we had played for the Howler. I looked in the great memory pool for some memory of what had occurred on the Iskoort planet. Nothing. Some memory of us, of five humans and an Andalite and a Chee and Guide. But there was nothing.

Crayak had destroyed the six remaining Howlers before those memories could poison the minds of all Howlers. He'd done what I knew — what I had hoped — he'd do.

The Howlers had never been defeated. So they believed, but I knew that wasn't possible. Somewhere, somehow, someone had to have beaten them, at least once. Perfection was impossible.

So if the collective memory had no trace of defeat, it could only mean that Crayak had destroyed his defeated Howlers before the memory of failure could infect them all.

He might have done that many times over the millennia. Always keeping the Howlers' collective memory from any taint that might weaken their innocent evil.

He had no choice. A collective memory was very useful for spreading battle tactics and experience. But it was a weakness, too. Crayak could not allow his murderous children to learn one simple fact: that their victims were not part of a game, but real people, with dreams and hopes and loves.

Crayak had acted quickly. The memories of humans and Andalites, Chee, and Iskoort had not been allowed to infect the Howler memory. Nothing had gotten through . . .

No. Not nothing!

Sifting through the collective memory, through the unbroken chain of horror, I caught a single fugitive image, like a few seconds of film.

Just the picture of Cassie running to me, and our arms and lips and . . .

I demorphed back to human. And when I had my own mouth again, I said, "You were too late, Crayak. Something got through to the Howlers' collective memory."

"What?" he demanded.

"Love."

CHAPTER 27

We were no longer with Crayak. We were back in that weird, n-dimensional space where inside was outside and nothing made any sense at all.

Still, it was good to be away from Crayak.

Good to be alive.

"You did well," the Ellimist said.

"Did well? Did *well*?" Marco echoed. "We kicked butt on the meanest gang in the galaxy, whupped Crayak the Big Nasty, saved the Iskoort, which I'm still not sure was a good thing, and planted a little sensitivity time bomb in the Howlers, and that's it? 'Job well done,' and 'Oh, by the way, here's your insides to look at again as we zip through inside-out world'?"

143

"What would you like?" the Ellimist asked reasonably.

"I don't know. How about a reward or something?"

"How about telling us what we accomplished, if anything?" I said.

"Yeah," Rachel agreed. "How about that?"

Suddenly, without any warning, we were back in Cassie's barn. Right where we'd been the instant before the Ellimist had whisked us off to the Iskoort planet.

"What did you accomplish? No one knows the future. Not for certain. But it is now more likely than it was before that three hundred years from now the Yeerks will encounter the Iskoort. They will realize that they are related. And the Yeerks will see that there is a better way."

<That's it?> Tobias asked. <Three centuries from now? How does that help us?>

"It doesn't," the Ellimist said. "But within six months Crayak will send a Howler force to annihilate a race called the Sharf Den. Instead of slaughtering the Sharf Den, the Howlers will try something different." The Ellimist winked. "They will attempt to kiss them. Crayak will have lost his shock troops. And the Sharf Den will . . . well, no one knows the future for certain. Oh, however, you may be sure that Guide is now a very, very rich Iskoort."

With a laugh of pure pleasure, the Ellimist was gone.

<I really hate when he does that,> Tobias said.

"Okay, that does it, we're never inviting him over again," Marco said.

It was good winning one. A big one.

And that night, when I fell asleep, the eye of Crayak was no longer in my dreams.

Instead I dreamed about Cassie. But in my dreams I also saw that Howler, falling and falling beside me. Falling still, as I spread my wings and split my fate from his.

Marco's always saying you choose how to see the world. That you can look at what's funny and cool, or you can focus on all the things that aren't.

So I tried to follow Marco's advice. I tried to turn my dreams to Cassie.

But even looking into her eyes, I still saw that doomed Howler falling.

I've mentioned that morphs get weird? That things don't happen in some nice, neat, gradual way? Well, this morph was ridiculous.

I was growing, growing, growing! My skin had turned leathery graphite-gray. There was a blow-hole in the back of my neck. My head was monstrous and out of proportion.

But the rest of me was still Rachel. I had a head the size of Iowa. And about an acre of floating blonde hair.

<Oh, man!> Marco groaned. <Oh, I didn't need to see this! Rachel, you have pores as big as potholes!>

<This is ridiculous,> Jake complained. <I am tangled in your hair!>

<She's sinking!> Ax said. <Her buoyancy has not adjusted. She has dense human tissues.>

<I do not,> I said, vaguely offended. But he was right: I was sinking.

And if I didn't finish morphing, I was going to drown. Probably sink to the bottom and float past the Pemalite ship. A big, drowned, female Gulliver.

That got me back on track. . . .

I bobbed to the surface. My blowhole inhaled. My lungs filled.

I felt the water ripple as the dolphins surged and danced.

I sensed their joy and felt a deep, thousand-generation-old kinship with my lithe, sleek brethren.

I drew a deep breath, expanding my lungs to their full capacity, and dove, arching my dorsal hump and flipping my triangular fluke into the air.

I fired off a blast of pulsed clicks and received a "picture" of everything around me. Like a black-and-white sketch that traced across my mind and was erased like an Etch-A-Sketch.

I was echolocating. I had natural sonar.

I "saw" the dolphins and they "saw" me.

And then another large creature was moving toward me.

<Rachel, I sure hope that's you,> Tobias called.

Oh. Right.

The whale brain wasn't hard to control.

The thing was, I hadn't even tried.

I'd liked the calm confidence. The absence of fear.

<It's definitely me,> I said, rolling and powering my gigantic, muscled body up, up, up toward dim light like a runaway train.

Another train rushed beside me. We raced to the barrier between sky and sea.

<Yah-HAH!> Tobias shouted as we exploded the barrier and erupted into the sky. Our massive heads surged into the crisp air, water shimmering down around us.

<Okay, that was cool,> Jake said.

<I wanna be a sperm whale,> Marco whined.

<I don't think so,> Jake said. <Tick-tock. We need to stay on track here.>

<Just need to suck some air,> I said.

I exhaled, spouting spray and drawing in enough air to last to maximum dive capacity. Passages in my massive head filled with water and, all automatically, the waxy deposits of spermaceti cooled the water and sent me plunging.

Into giant squid territory. I hoped.

Where the atmospheric pressure could squeeze every last molecule of air from a human body.

<Ready, Rachel?> Tobias asked.

<Ready,> I said, sighing and shivering deep in my soul. The whale might not be scared. I was.

You have been **chosen...**

Are you ready?

If you've ever wished you could join the Animorphs...

Now's your chance.

Coming to bookstores in March!